CASEY WOOSTER'S PET CARE SERVICE

CASEY WOOSTER'S

PET CARE SERVICE

BY JANET NICHOLS

Atheneum   1993   New York

Maxwell Macmillan Canada
Toronto

Maxwell Macmillan International
New York   Oxford   Singapore   Sydney

Atheneum
Macmillan Publishing Company
866 Third Avenue
New York, NY 10022

Maxwell Macmillan Canada, Inc.
1200 Eglinton Avenue East
Suite 200
Don Mills, Ontario M3C 3N1

Macmillan Publishing Company is part of the
Maxwell Communication Group of Companies.

First edition
Printed in the United States of America
10 9 8 7 6 5 4 3 2 1
The text of this book is set in 12 point Goudy Old Style.
Book design by Tania Garcia.
Library of Congress Cataloging-in-Publication Data

Nichols, Janet, 1952–
Casey Wooster's pet care service / Janet Nichols. — 1st ed.
p.   cm.
Summary: When eleven-year-old Casey comes up with a plan to earn
money so she can visit her mother in Los Angeles, she also gets to
know her stepbrother and stepmother better.
ISBN 0-689-31879-0
[1. Stepfamilies—Fiction. 2. Moneymaking projects—Fiction.
3. Mothers and daughters—Fiction.] I. Title.
PZ7.N5365Cas 1993
[Fic]—dc20   93-7041

*To Timothy
with love*

CONTENTS

CASEY WOOSTER'S PET CARE SERVICE

Chapter 1
Bad News

I was real excited about spending the summer with my mom. She's an actress and she lives in Beverly Hills. Actually, it's Sherman Oaks, near Beverly Hills. Actually, she's *trying* to be an actress. She works at Jiffy Lube changing the oil in people's cars. She has to spend a lot of time taking her fingernails on and off—long, red fake ones that go on top of her stubby real ones, which are outlined in black grease that won't wash off. She says she'll get her big acting break soon.

On the night of the last day of school Mom called me with the bad news. "Hi, hon, it's me. I gotta make it short."

"I know," I said. My mom used to talk to me on the phone so much that her bill got sky high and the telephone company took her phone away. Now she has to use other people's phones and talk fast.

"Look, Casey, I know this is a big disappointment, but you can't come visit right now. I don't have the cash for your airline ticket. Don't worry, though. Something will come up. I almost got to be the tomato in a salad dressing commercial today." Mom said she was real sorry over and over until someone in the background told her to hang up.

After I got off the phone, I explained the situation to my dad. "Can't you buy my airline ticket?" I asked.

"Absolutely not," he said. "This is your mom's responsibility. It's high time she started accepting some."

I hate that word *responsibility*. Parents are always finding new ways to use it against you. "That's just an excuse," I said to Dad. "You don't want to spend any money on me either. You just want to wreck my whole summer."

"Aw now, Casey, it won't be wrecked," he said. "You can have fun at home with Mollie, Benjamin, and me."

"Some fun," I said. "About as fun as plastic dog poop." I ran upstairs to my room and slammed the door.

Mollie is my stepmother and Benjamin is my stepbrother. Mollie and Dad got married about a year ago. They bought this house in Carmichael, a suburb of Sacramento, which is the capital of California, which you probably already know if you've been to fifth grade.

Dad tells people I've had trouble adjusting and it's no wonder. It's pretty weird when some yucky lady your dad has been dating suddenly moves in on you and starts thinking she's your mom. I had a perfectly good mom already. And I thought someday I might even get a brother, but I expected him to start out as a baby who would look up to me. Benjamin looks up to me, all right, because he's such a shrimp. But he's only one year younger than me and he's super smart. He skipped fourth grade, which put us in fifth grade together. The kids at our new school kept asking if we were twins— gross! Sticking out the school year with Mollie and Benjamin was bad enough. It was no fair having to hang around with them all summer, too.

I went to my desk and started writing:

Dear Mom,

I know you really hate me. First you run away from home and now you don't want me to visit you. You don't want me to have any fun. It's all your fault I'm living with the mother of someone else's kid instead of you. And if I was supposed to have a brother you should have stayed home with me and Dad and given birth to a boy. Then we would have all lived together happily ever after.

Instead I am miserable. I haven't seen you since Christmas. That's a long time for an eleven-year-old. I'm a lot different now with a longer ponytail plus I know fractions sort of. You are missing my whole life. Probably the next time I see you I will be as old as you are now and you won't even recognize me like in that made-for-TV movie you told me to watch because you almost got the part of the grown-up daughter. Now I know you really and truly don't care about me.

Your one and only child who
loves you even if you don't love her,
Casey Wooster

That last part really choked me up. My tears dropped onto the paper and blurred the words. One, two, three tears.

I tried to space them out evenly so it would look like I had been writing and crying. I made a game of trying to bomb certain words with my tears. I looked at the word *love* and I thought: Ready, aim, fire. I missed. I moved my head over *movie*. Ready, aim, fire. Yes! A hit! That made me smile.

I ducked down and wiped my eyes on my T-shirt. I spotted my packed suitcase on the floor next to my bed. Inside it were three presents from my mom: an official Dodgers baseball cap to wear when we went to Dodgers' games; an automatic-focus camera to take pictures at Disneyland; and a Marilyn Monroe towel to lie on at Santa Monica Beach. I wondered if all that stuff added up to one airline ticket from Sacramento to Los Angeles. Maybe my mom shouldn't have bought it all.

Dad says Mom isn't so good with money—she goes through it like water. Of course Dad and Mollie are excellent with money. They are "in finance," meaning they work in banks. They just love to work with money and talk about money and invest money. So does Benjamin. I am more like my mom. I never think about money unless I want real bad to buy something.

Now I was thinking hard about how to earn some. I couldn't baby-sit because Jenny, my own baby-sitter, wouldn't let me. I couldn't do housework because I'm not that good at it, plus if somebody asked me to clean their toilet I'd probably barf. I couldn't take care of anybody's pool because people would worry that I would fall in, which would be no problem because I can swim pretty well, at least dog-paddle.

When I thought of the word *dog* it felt like lightning had struck inside my brain. I snapped my fingers. That's it! I could walk people's dogs. I could brush people's big furry cats. I could go into the pet care business. It would be a perfect business for me because when I grow up I want to be a veterinarian—a *big*-animal veterinarian, meaning horses. I'm just crazy about horses. Someday I'm going to have one of my very own. I'm not going to mess around with cats and dogs, but they would be an okay place to start.

I wadded up my letter to my mom and threw it into the wastebasket. It was so soggy it would take extra stamps to send. Plus I wasn't mad or sad anymore. No more tears for me, I had a plan. I started another letter:

Dear Mom,

Too bad you didn't have the money to buy my airline ticket. Don't worry, I understand. I know how hard it is for you to earn a living and try to be an actress. I'm sorry you didn't get the part of the tomato in the salad dressing commercial. Probably they were looking for someone fat with a sunburn. You'll probably get the starring role in a movie any day now. I miss you and I know you miss me, too.

Love, your daughter,
Casey Wooster

I felt much better after that. I put on my pajamas, washed my face, and brushed my teeth without Dad or Mollie telling me to. I got into bed, but I didn't sleep. I was too excited about my new pet care service. This is my best thinking time, when I'm lying in the quiet dark, halfway between being awake and being asleep. My brain really stretches out and grabs all sorts of neat ideas that it usually can't reach during the day. I think my brain goes on working on these ideas, even when I'm asleep and dreaming.

In the morning some of my night ideas seem really stupid, and I'm glad nobody but me knows I thought of them. But *some* of my sleepy ideas are really cool!

Chapter 2

Going into Business

I was up early the next morning so I could get on the computer before Benjamin. He wasn't too happy about that. He slumped down on the sofa to wait his turn. He opened the *Wall Street Journal*, but I don't think he got much reading done. I could feel his squinty little eyes hitting me right between the shoulder blades.

I selected a lemon-yellow piece of construction paper, fed it into the printer, and pressed P.

Brizzzzzz zit zit, zit, brizzzz.

"Hey, what are you printing out?" Benjamin asked.

"None of your beeswax."

In a flash he was at my side, lunging for the paper. I tried slapping my hand over it, but he was too fast for me. Benjamin held the paper two inches from his contact lens-coated eyeballs. Most ten-year-olds are too young to wear contacts, but Benjamin is exceptionally responsible. Just ask his mother, she'll tell you.

He read aloud, "Casey Wooster's Pet Care and Grooming Service. My house is your pet's hotel. Relax on your vacation and leave the pet walking to me. Quality, super-plus care from a future big-animal veterinarian. Call 555–0867." He let go of the paper and it floated to the tabletop. "What are you trying to raise money for?"

"None of your beeswax." I like to keep him in the dark as much as possible. I fed a shocking-pink piece of paper into the printer and pressed P.

"It's for a horse, right?"

"Maybe yes, maybe no."

"You'll never raise the capital, even if you make the right investments. Interest rates are at rock bottom."

"Hmm." I fanned out my construction paper and pressed my forefinger against my cheek, pretending like my next color selection took every brain cell I had.

"Okay, so it's not a horse," said Benjamin.

I decided to give him ten seconds. I thought to myself: one Mississippi, two Mississippi, three Mississippi . . .

"Even if you were able to raise the cash to go see your mom, what makes you think the front office would let you?" The front office is what Benjamin calls our parents . . . well, my father, his mother. Actually I hadn't thought about needing their permission. "You worry too far in advance," I said.

Benjamin tapped my flier. "I bet you haven't cleared this nifty little operation with the front office either."

"Nope. Are you going to tell on me?"

He straightened indignantly, causing his white-blond cowlick to wave like an alien's antenna. "I am not a tattletale!"

I turned toward Benjamin, pivoting my chin on my palm, slowly, for dramatic effect. I raised my eyebrows so high they scraped my black, frizzy bangs.

Benjamin's chipmunk cheeks turned red as cherry tomatoes. "Okay, so sometimes I get you busted, but not every time. That would mean spending too much time with the front office. How are you going to explain the sudden appearance of a dog in our backyard? Or cat? Or boa constrictor?"

"For all your bulging brains, you don't know a thing about parent psychology," I said. "If I marched right up to Dad and Mollie this morning and asked them if I could start a pet care service, they'd give me a flat-out no. But if I go ahead with my plan and they find out later, they might say, okay, maybe."

"Hey, cool," said Benjamin. "Can I help?"

"Nope."

"Oh, come on, Casey, please."

"No way."

"Hey, look. I could handle the paperwork."

"Well . . . okay."

"Gee, thanks," said Benjamin. "You won't regret this."

Actually I wanted his help, but I like to see him grovel first. I don't like to do stuff alone that much and all my friends are spending the summer at camp or with the parent they don't usually live with. Benjamin's dad was riding his bike around the world, so obviously Benjamin wouldn't be seeing him for a while.

"What's my cut?" he asked.

"Your cut? I figured you'd pay *me* for letting you in on all the fun."

"Ha ha, so funny I forgot to laugh."

"Okay," I said. "We'll split our earnings fifty-fifty."

"Wow. I never expected to come in as a full partner. That's very generous, Case."

"I know," I said coolly. Actually I didn't know how to figure out percents, but I could divide by two. I nodded toward my growing stack of fliers. "I'm keeping the company name the way it is though."

"Hey, that's okay. It wouldn't be cost-time effective to change it. I don't mind being a silent partner. If we get busted, then you'll have to take most of the heat."

The whole time we were arguing, I kept printing out fliers. We had a whole stack by the time Dad burst into the family room. He always does things in bursts because he's an exercise nut. He was dressed for work, his suit jacket slung over his shoulder, his briefcase under his arm. He has a crew cut that goes all haywire because his black hair is as kinky as mine. I get my dark brown eyes and pointed chin from him, too. In fact people say I'm the spitting image of him. I'd like to know what spit has to do with it. It sort of grosses me out just thinking up possibilities.

Mollie was right behind Dad. She was wearing her navy boxlike suit with a flouncy bow at the neck that always reminds me of a Christmas present, the kind filled with underwear and socks.

"What are you kids doing cooped up indoors on the first beautiful day of summer vacation?" Dad crossed the room in three long strides. He pulled opened the drapes, causing us to blink in the bright sunlight.

Benjamin squinted into the monitor like he was trying to solve some deep mystery of the universe. His forearms rested over our stack of fliers.

I flipped off the computer and said, "We were just going for a walk."

Dad faked an astonished look. "At the same time? In the same direction? On the same side of the street?"

"Don't wander too far," Mollie said. "Your sitter is going to be a little late this morning."

"Jenny's no baby-sitter," said Dad. "We hired her to referee. Now, if she doesn't show up in regulation zebra stripes and a whistle, I want to hear about it."

"Oh, Daddy," I said. He's always saying corny stuff like that and trying to pass it off as funny.

"Casey, you're wearing your new jeans," said Mollie. "I was hoping you'd save them for good."

"Then they'll get too little for me so fast I'll only get to wear them about two times. You're just not used to being around a kid that grows."

"Hey, I'm not that shrimpy," said Benjamin.

The sides of Mollie's mouth pushed out, but the middle part didn't budge. She fakes smiles at me a lot. It makes her little white face look mousier than usual. Sometimes I think Dad made a list of all the things Mom is—pretty, warm, fun, etc.—and decided to go after a second wife who is the exact opposite. "Please change the pants, Casey."

"Okay, okay."

"Hey, Ben, would you mow the back-back today?" Dad asked.

"Sure."

Our backyard is a half acre divided by a fence. The front part is our formal backyard, with a patio, lawn, and flower beds. The back part is the back-back. It used to be part of a walnut orchard. There are a few big old trees left and the rest is just weeds. Everyone sort of forgets all about it until it starts looking like a jungle.

"We wouldn't need to mow the back-back if I got a horse," I said.

Dad held up his palms. "We're not getting into that subject now. I'm already running late."

Mollie checked her gold wristwatch. "Me, too. Oh, kids, I've got some salmon thawing out on the counter. Will one of you put it in the refrigerator in a few hours?"

"Fish again?" I said. "How come we all have to suffer just because you're on a diet?"

"If you learn good eating habits now, Casey, you won't have a weight problem later like me."

"Aw, you're not a bit fat," I said. "Anyway, you look good enough to me."

"Thank you, Casey," said Mollie, "but the important thing is how I feel about myself."

I should have known "good enough" would never be good enough for Mollie. She had to be perfect.

Everyone said good-bye and Dad and Mollie left. I gathered up the fliers and Benjamin got the thumbtacks out of the kitchen drawer. We went out the front door, leaving it unlocked for Jenny. Out on the street, we began tacking up the fliers on every telephone pole we came to. The job went fast. We had only one flier left when we came to a telephone pole that was mostly covered by a bush.

"Let's just skip it," said Benjamin.

"I don't want to skip it," I said. "This might be our lucky pole. We might get a ton of customers off it." I nodded toward a white picket fence. "I'll just stand on this and tack the flier up higher. We might be putting these things down too low for adults to read anyway."

The pickets were on the outside of the fence and a little ledge was on the inside. I thought about climbing over the pickets, but they could tear my new jeans. I had been in too big a hurry to change them. I spotted a gate around the corner of the fence. I walked up the driveway and swung open the gate.

"Hey, that's trespassing!" Benjamin shouted.

"No one will care." I started across the yard. A dog barked from behind the house. "Hey, cool," I said. "They even have a dog. Maybe it needs to be walked."

Just then a brown scruffy mutt streaked down the side of the house like a bullet aimed at me.

"Yikers!" I yelled. I bolted toward the fence, leaped onto the ledge, and hugged the telephone pole for balance. I felt a hard tug on my pant leg and heard the material rip. I looked down. The little brown beast was suspended a foot off the ground. Two of his yellow fangs were poking through the hem of my jeans. His fierce black eyes glared at me. I didn't know it then, but I was face to face with our first customer.

Chapter 3

Our First Customer

A woman came out of the house and called, "Don't be scared, little girl. Ferdie won't bite."

I looked down at the dog, his jaws still clamped to my pants, his hind legs kicking the air. Mollie says adults don't like kids to contradict them so I didn't say anything.

The woman started walking across the yard. She was wearing a fuchsia muumuu with big flowers all over it and those pink sponge curlers women used in the olden days before hot rollers were invented. The dog let go of my pants and ran to meet his owner. He leaped up and nipped at her frayed pocket. The woman withdrew a doggie treat and popped it in the air. The dog's jaws snapped it up.

I jumped over the fence onto the sidewalk. The hole in my pant leg caught on a picket. Fortunately, the material ripped free and I was able to land feet first. The damage was done to my pants instead of my head.

"Are you hurt?" the woman asked me.

"I'm fine," I said, though I knew I wouldn't be when Mollie saw my pants. "My *best* jeans aren't so good though." I figured if I whined a little she might offer to pay for them.

Then Benjamin ruined it for me. "I'm sorry my sister trespassed in your yard and upset your dog, Mrs. . . . uh . . ."

"Emma Beasel."

"Mrs. Beasel. Pleased to meet you." Benjamin poked his hand between the pickets. The dog lunged for it. Benjamin jerked his hand away.

"Ferdie won't bite you," Mrs. Beasel said again. "He just thinks you have a treat for him." She reached in her pocket and tossed the dog another morsel. He was a little roly-poly. In fact, both he and Mrs. Beasel seemed to do too much snacking.

Benjamin continued the formal introductions. "I'm Benjamin True and this is my sister, Casey Wooster."

"Stepsister," I said. "We're not related, not really."

"But it must be nice for you to have a little playmate in your own family," Mrs. Beasel said.

"Little is right."

"I'm not that little," said Benjamin.

I was about to argue back. Then I remembered Mollie saying people shouldn't take personal problems into the workplace. "Actually, my dad says we're doing pretty good for two 'onlys' thrown together in the middle of our formative years."

Mrs. Beasel rolled back her head and hooted. Adults are always laughing when I expect it the least. It's embarrassing. "What can I do for you?" she asked.

"Not a thing," said Benjamin, his eyes darting nervously over the dog. "We're sorry to have disturbed you."

Mrs. Beasel's black eyebrows had a head-on collision over her nose. "Weren't you about to knock on my door?"

"Oh, no," I said. "I just needed to borrow your fence to stand on, so I could tack up this flier." I handed it to Mrs. Beasel. "If you ever need someone to take care of old Ferdie here, just give us a buzz."

She bent her head over the flier. Benjamin twisted his head like he was watching a Ping-Pong tournament. (No, he did not want to take care of Ferdie.) I bounced my head like I was watching a dribbling basketball. (Yes, we needed the business.) Benjamin bared his teeth and pretended to lunge at my arm and shook his head again. I shrugged and looked away. If Mrs. Beasel said Ferdie wouldn't bite, he probably wouldn't bite—hard.

"My house is your pet's hotel," Mrs. Beasel read aloud. "How very sweet. As a matter of fact, I'm leaving this afternoon to spend two weeks with my sister in Missoura. Too bad I already made arrangements for Ferdie at the kennel."

"The kennel!" I exclaimed. "Don't they keep animals cooped up in little cages without giving them any exercise?"

"Or treats," said Mrs. Beasel. "Ferdie comes out of there looking like he's been in a concentration camp."

"No love and attention either," I said. "We could give Ferdie plenty of that. And our back-back has tons of room to run around in. It's about a half acre."

"It's more like a quarter, Case," said Benjamin.

"Ferdie is used to sleeping in my bed," said Mrs. Beasel.

"We can bring him indoors at night," I said.

"Well, then, how much experience have you had?"

"None whatsoever," said Benjamin. "Our parents won't let us have pets."

"But I know what to do," I said. "I've read lots of books about it. I know a dog needs plenty of clean fresh water, a soft place to sleep, exercise, brushing, baths, and, oh, all kinds of stuff."

"I'm afraid know-how is no substitute for practical experience," said Mrs. Beasel. "Ferdie is an AKC-registered miniature poodle. His full name is King Ferdinand the Sixth. His great-great-grandfather, King Ferdinand the Third, was a three-time reigning county champion."

My jaw dropped so low I was afraid it would come unhinged like a snake's. "Are you sure?"

Mrs. Beasel's eyebrows had another train wreck. "I must admit he doesn't look much like a champion now. I don't keep him clipped like a poodle anymore. He's quite elderly and the shears make him jittery. He hasn't been in a dog show for seven years. Not since Mr. Beasel, God rest his soul, passed away." She looked real sad and lonely.

Benjamin said, "What my sister meant is: *Are you sure* you would even consider having us kids take care of such a valuable pedigree?"

Mrs. Beasel pursed her lips, looking like a fish on a hook. Now all we had to do was reel her in. "What are your rates?" she asked.

"Two dollars a day," I blurted.

"She means three," said Benjamin.

"How reasonable," said Mrs. Beasel. "The kennel charges twice as much."

"Plus food," said Benjamin.

"Oh, I have plenty of food," said Mrs. Beasel. "I'll send it along with you."

"You mean we got the job?" I asked.

"Yes, Casey, you most certainly do. You and Benjamin seem to be very sincere young people. And very responsible."

She flipped a doggie treat off her thumbnail as if it were a quarter. Ferdie snapped it up in midair. His jaws sounded like a steel trap slamming shut. Benjamin squeezed his eyes closed and shuddered.

Chapter 4
Wierd Wilbur Burr

After Mrs. Beasel gave us plenty of instructions and supplies, we headed for home. Benjamin lugged a grocery sack full of canned food, dry food, dog biscuits, and boxes and boxes of doggie treats. I held on to a leash linked to another leash linked to Ferdie. Every few steps, I dug into an opened box of doggie treats and tossed one over my shoulder. Ferdie paused to slurp up each morsel as it dropped.

"Hey, stop feeding that dog," said Benjamin.

"Wouldn't you rather have him eat doggie treats than take a bite out of your ankle?"

"I'll take my chances." He snatched the box of treats from me and stuck it in the bag. "Overfeeding is bad for him."

"Mrs. Beasel does it."

"Yeah, and she's killing him. She fools herself into thinking it won't really hurt him."

"She probably likes to see him happy," I said. "It's cute the way his little ears perk up when he's happy."

"Nothing's cute about this mutt," said Benjamin.

"Not how he looks. How he acts. Sometimes you have to get to know someone before they look good to you."

We walked a little farther before Benjamin spoke again. "Aren't you afraid of what the front office is going to say?"

"You worry too much. What do you think—that they'll make us ship Ferdie off to Missoura?"

"Missour-*ee*." Benjamin shifted his load. "I say Ferdie is one big mistake."

"Oh, it'll be fun to take care of him. A dog isn't as good as a horse, but at least we get to have an animal live at our house for a while." We reached our street, Barnett Circle. Benjamin started to go around to the right, but I turned around, heading back to Mendota.

"Where are you going, now?" said Benjamin. "My arms are about to drop off."

"I want to go by the Burrs's."

"The Burrs's!" Benjamin stopped in his tracks. He showed white all around his eyeballs. "Are you crazy?"

"You remember how Mrs. Burr hemmed up that skirt of Mollie's? Well, I want to ask her if she'll patch my jeans. The worst thing that can happen is she'll say no."

"A lot worse can happen if you ask me," said Benjamin.

We had gotten a pretty bad scare at the Burrs's last Halloween. On their porch, sitting in the shadows, was a figure wearing a floppy patchwork hat, leopard fake-fur jacket, and yellow suede pants. We figured something dressed that weird had to be a scarecrow. Then it jumped out of the chair to hand us candy bars and we about jumped out of our skins! We screamed and ran while the Burrs's grown-up son Wilbur bellowed, "Har, har, har."

I knew that was what Benjamin was thinking about. "Go on home then, scaredy-cat." I headed toward the Burrs's.

Benjamin hesitated, then reluctantly trudged after me. I knew he would. In front of the Burrs's we paused on the sidewalk and stared up at their house. The roof sagged, the paint was peeling off the sides, and the lawn was mostly dead weeds. There was nothing scary about that on a sunny morning, but the spot on my neck underneath my ponytail felt like an ice cube was pressed up against it.

I took a deep breath and we started up the walkway. I saw Mrs. Burr seated at the window in the front bedroom. The sewing machine light was on and her head was bent over her work. We walked up the steps and I rang the doorbell. The Burrs's front door was open and we could see through the screen. I know it's not polite to peep into other people's houses, but sometimes my curiosity gets the best of me. It was real messy. Against one wall were two stacks of newspapers that almost touched the ceiling.

"They must never throw anything out," I whispered. I pressed the doorbell again.

"Yeah, and it stinks in there." Benjamin wrinkled his nose. "Stale cigarette smoke . . . and something else."

"Bacon grease."

Benjamin scrunched up his face and took a couple of short sniffs. "And something else."

"Kitty litter!"

"Used kitty litter," said Benjamin. "Used a lot."

"Maybe they'll hire us to clean it every day."

"You can clean it," said Benjamin. "I'm beating it out of here. She's not going to answer."

I took a step back and glanced toward the front bedroom window. "She's still sewing. Maybe she thinks we're selling something and—"

"Whatdda you kids want?" said a gruff voice behind the screen door.

We both jumped. Ferdie let out a wounded howl.

Wilbur poked his head out of the screen door. I'm not good at judging ages of adults, but I knew he was too old to still be living with his parents. He already had a bald spot. Right next to his nose was a mole in the shape of a three-leaf clover, with a long hair coming out like a stem.

I tried to meet his eyes, but I couldn't stop staring at the mole. Something that ugly smack in the middle of someone's face is hard to ignore. "May I . . . may we speak to your mother?" I asked.

"She's busy," he snapped. "Whatdda you want with her?"

"I was wondering if she could fix my jeans." I raised my leg to show Wilbur the ripped cuff.

"She's no professional seamstress. She just sews for the family." Wilbur was wearing a lavender suit made out of thick spongy material people used to wear in the olden days. The coat had a collar like a shirt's pinned onto it.

"Who is it, Sonny?" Mrs. Burr called out.

"No one, Ma," said Wilbur. "Just the Wooster kids."

"What do they want?" Mrs. Burr's voice sounded right behind her son.

"Nothing. They were just leaving." Wilbur started to close the door, but Mrs. Burr straight-armed it. She only came up to her son's chin. She had wiry gray hair and a big bosom. She always wore an apron like Mrs. Santa Claus.

"Please, Mrs. Burr, could you patch my jeans?" I asked. "I just ripped them and they're brand new."

"Of course, dear," said Mrs. Burr. "Go home and change, and bring them back. I'll toss them in my heap of mending."

I had a feeling once something got tossed in a heap of anything in that house it was lost forever. "I really sort of need them today," I said.

"Oh, I need to finish Sonny's new leisure suit today."

"Oh, okay, then, never mind," I said. "Just one other thing. We happened to . . . um . . . notice your cat box and—"

"You kids been snooping around the back of the house?" Wilbur cut in.

"No!" I said. "We just uh . . . well, we sort of smelled it out here. Maybe you'd like to hire us to come over and scoop it out every day."

"We can take care of our own animals," said Wilbur.

"We are going to be spending a few days at Granny's— I mean, my mother's," said Mrs. Burr. "Perhaps you can feed our cats while we're away."

"That would be great," I said, ignoring the little coughing sounds Benjamin was making. "When do you need us?"

"Let's see. We're leaving tomorrow morning and we'll be

home Sunday night. The cats eat just once a day, so you'll only have to come by three times. How much would that be?"

"Nine dollars, ma'am," said Benjamin, springing to life at the mention of money.

"Highway robbery," said Wilbur. "Forget it, Ma. I'm staying home. We need someone here to take care of things."

I didn't dare look at Benjamin for fear we'd both crack up. It didn't seem like anyone took care of anything around there, ever.

"Of course, you're going, Sonny," said Mrs. Burr, twisting around to tap him lightly on the wrist. "Granny would be so disappointed not to see her big boy. Come in, kids. I'll show you what to do."

Wilbur turned and stomped toward the back of the house. Pretty soon we heard a door slam. I guess he went to hide out in his room like a little kid who didn't get his own way.

Benjamin tied Ferdie's leash to the porch railing and we stepped inside. It stunk so bad I was dying to hold my nose.

Mrs. Burr led us through the living room to the kitchen. She showed us where the cats' food and water dishes and litter box were. She fished in her purse for her keys and removed one of them from the ring. "This goes to the back door," she said, handing it to me. She wrote something on a slip of paper and gave it to Benjamin. "And here's my mother's phone number in case of an emergency."

I thought everything was taken care of, but then Benjamin asked, "Where are your cats, Mrs. Burr?"

"Oh! They skedaddle when strangers come around. I'll

round them up for you." Mrs. Burr went into the living room and got down on her hands and knees to look under the sofa. "Here, Boo!" She got up and peered around one of the stacks of newspapers. "Come on, Spooky! Kitty, kitty!" Her arm nudged the newspapers and the whole stack began to sway. I raised my eyebrows to my bangs and held my breath, but then the tower of newspapers stopped teetering.

"Well, they're here someplace," said Mrs. Burr. "Boo is all black and skinny and Spooky is black, too, but a little fatter with a longer tail. I can tell them apart, but Wilbur and Pop have trouble unless they see them together. You'll see what I mean. They'll come running when they hear you scraping out their cat food tomorrow night."

"Night!" cried Benjamin. "What do you mean 'night'?"

"Oh, dear, didn't I mention that we feed our cats at bedtime?" said Mrs. Burr. "I suppose your parents don't let you out after dark."

"Don't worry, Mrs. Burr," I said. "Your cats are used to eating at night, we'll come at night."

She led us to the front door and we said good-bye. I untied Ferdie, Benjamin took up the load of dog food, and we scurried toward home like a bogeyman was on our tail.

"No way I'm going into that creepy house after dark," said Benjamin.

"We'll go right after dinner," I said. "It will be plenty light. They'll all be gone, including weird Wilbur."

"It was smart of Mrs. Burr to give us a phone number in case of an emergency. Maybe we should go back to Mrs. Beasel's and get a number where she can be reached, too."

I didn't want to go back and give Mrs. Beasel a chance to change her mind about us taking care of Ferdie. "What could happen?" I asked.

Benjamin shrugged. He looked too tired to answer.

I got to thinking about Wilbur Burr some more. "Why would anybody put two 'burrs' in one kid's name?"

"It fits," said Benjamin, and we both laughed.

I pressed my forefinger against the side of my nose. "You know that thing on his face? I wonder if he's lucky."

"Huh?" asked Benjamin. "No, Case, it's a *four*-leaf clover that's supposed to be lucky."

"Oh, I knew that," I said. "I just forgot."

Chapter 5
Mollie Meets Ferdie

When we got home we showed Ferdie around the back-back. He sniffed each and every walnut tree and wet a few of them. Benjamin kept him company while I went into the garage to look for supplies.

In the plastic recycling bin I found two cottage cheese containers for his food and water bowls. I thought about using the chaise lounge pad or a sleeping bag for his bed, but I knew Dad and Mollie wouldn't like either idea. Then I spotted my old doll crib. I hadn't played with it in ages, which is probably why it landed out in the garage. I tucked it under my arm and went out to the back-back.

I handed the plastic containers to Benjamin and set the crib down under a tree. I patted the mattress. "Here you go, Ferdie. Nap time."

Ferdie perked up his ears but didn't budge.

"Well, try it," I coaxed. "It's nice and soft."

Ferdie just stared at me.

"Maybe it looks too closed in," said Benjamin.

I took the mattress out of the crib and fluffed up the doll quilt. Ferdie sniffed at the bedding. Benjamin picked up the garden hose, turned on the faucet, and filled one of the containers with fresh water. Ferdie sniffed at that, too. He looked at the empty container, then back up at me.

"Aw, he's hungry," I said. "Couldn't we give him just a little dry food so he knows his new place comes with eats?"

"Absolutely not."

I held out my empty palms to Ferdie. "Sorry, boy."

Ferdie seemed to take no for an answer. He got up on the mattress, walked around in two circles going one way, turned, and walked around in another circle going the other way. His legs collapsed and his chin came to rest on his haunches. He eyed the empty food container.

"Are you sure he'll be okay all alone out here?" I asked.

Benjamin nodded. "Come on, it's almost lunchtime."

Ferdie whimpered.

"Human lunchtime. Dogs don't eat lunch."

I elbowed Benjamin. "Stop mentioning the L word." I patted Ferdie's head. "Make yourself at home, now."

Benjamin and I walked out the gate. Ferdie watched us, but he didn't try to follow. We made sure the gate was latched and headed for the house. Inside, Benjamin went into the living room to say hi to Jenny while I ran upstairs before she could see my ripped pants. I changed into an old pair of jeans and hid my wrecked ones in the bottom of my winter clothes drawer.

Jenny fixed us some egg salad sandwiches for lunch. I got Benjamin laughing so hard that some of the egg stuff came out of his nose. Mollie would have had a cow, but Jenny thought it was funny. We like having her for a baby-sitter because she doesn't pay much attention to us. When our fights get real loud she comes around to check for blood, but the rest of the time she watches the soaps and talks on the phone.

After lunch I took Ferdie for a walk while Benjamin mowed the back-back. He spent the rest of the afternoon doing his most favorite thing in the whole world—reading. I tried to watch TV with Jenny, but this man and lady got into a long, disgusting kiss. I had to leave the room or barf. I played some computer games and checked on Ferdie a few times.

By four o'clock I was bored silly. I trudged up to my room and stood straight and stiff. "Timmmmmber!" I shouted, and crashed onto my bed. I lay there only a few seconds when my next brainstorm hit. I dashed into Benjamin's room.

"Hey, Benj, want to do something?"

"I already am." He didn't even look up from his book.

I sat on his bed and leaned over to get a closer look at the book cover. On it were some dead-looking hamsters on ice. "Eewee, sick. What's so interesting about hamster popsicles?"

Benjamin peered over his book. "A lot. This is about cryogenics—the effects produced by very low temperatures."

"Low temperatures freeze things," I said smugly. "I don't have to read a whole book to know that."

"It's not that simple," said Benjamin.

Now that I had his attention, I blurted out, "You know how Mrs. Beasel said Ferdie hasn't looked like a real poodle in seven years? Let's surprise her. Let's groom him."

"Oh, no, you don't. Mrs. Beasel said electric shears make Ferdie nervous—he'd probably bite us."

"Dad's electric razor is as quiet as a kitty-cat's purr."

Benjamin erupted with several loud beeps like a nuclear bomb warning. "Trouble alert! Trouble alert! Casey Wooster, about to get busted."

I snapped my fingers. "I got it! Instead of clipping the parts of Ferdie's fur that are supposed to be short, we can just slick them down with Mollie's hair mousse. For the curly parts, we can use her curling iron. It doesn't make any noise at all."

"Mom wouldn't like dog cooties on her curling iron."

"I knew it!" I crossed my arms. "The moment our business means real work, you want to bail out."

"This isn't about real work. It's about you wanting to play doggie beauty parlor." Benjamin was right, but I opened my mouth to protest. Before I could say anything he slammed the book shut. "But I can see I won't get a moment's peace until I cooperate."

"It'll be fun, Benj. You'll see. We'll skip the curling iron and just use mousse. I'll go get Ferdie. You get the *World Book* and open it to the poodle page. Meet you in my room in a flash."

I ran out to the back-back and got Ferdie. He was so glad to be let into the house, he danced in circles, his toenails making clicking sounds on the kitchen linoleum.

"What are you doing in there, Casey?" Jenny called from the living room.

"Nothing," I shouted back. I rustled a bag of banana chips to drown out Ferdie's tap dancing.

"Come here a sec," Jenny called.

I twisted the top part of my body around the doorframe and blocked Ferdie's way at the same time. "Yeah?"

"You and Benj have been awfully quiet this afternoon."

"Benjamin is reading and I'm just lying around."

"I might come and check on you anyway," said Jenny.

"Okay," I said, but I seriously doubted it. Jenny was painting her toenails. It was a very delicate operation. She was doing each nail in hot pink, fuchsia, and lime green stripes. Cotton balls were jammed in between her toes. She would have to climb the stairs balancing on her heels.

I gathered up Ferdie and dashed up the stairs. I made it to my room and shut the door behind me. Benjamin was sprawled on the floor reading the *World Book*. He wore his baseball glove on one hand and a pot holder mitt on the other.

"Hey, Case, did you know poodles originated in Germany in the 1500s?"

"Honestly! I leave you alone with a book one second and you're bound to come up with something educational. Here, let me see the picture. Hey, look at that cute little pom-pom at the tip of his tail. Let's try making that first."

I shook the can of mousse and squirted a mound into my left hand. Benjamin grabbed Ferdie's middle and I wrapped my right fist around his tail. He glared at me. A low growl gurgled deep in his throat. Benjamin and I let go quick and scooted back.

I studied the picture again. "Hey, look at that cute little curly topknot. Let's try making that first." Slowly, I reached out and patted Ferdie on the head. "There, there, good boy."

Benjamin clutched Ferdie again. I wrapped some topknot fur around my fingers and counted up to ten Mississippi, then unrolled the curl.

"Hey, it's straighter than before," said Benjamin.

"I can see that. Maybe I didn't hold it in long enough."

I rolled the fur up tighter. I stared at the second hand on my clock radio, thinking I would wait a full two minutes before releasing the curl. Time was just about up when Ferdie yelped and scampered under my bed. His topknot fur was sort of stiff and sort of gluey.

"You're really bugging him!" exclaimed Benjamin.

"I didn't mean to!"

"Well, he looks worse. Told you this was a dumb idea."

"Just shut up!" I rolled onto my belly and scooted under the bed. I spotted Ferdie back against the wall. I reached out for him. "Here, boy. I'm sorry I—*yow!*" I slithered away from him.

"Did he bite you?" exclaimed Benjamin.

I knelt back on my haunches and inspected the back of my stinging hand. The skin was puffing up around two blue puncture wounds. Tiny dots of blood were just beginning to surface. "It's not bad," I said, locking the pain behind clenched teeth. It always gets Benjamin how brave I can be.

"Benjamin! Casey! I'm home," Mollie called from downstairs.

"Oh, good," said Benjamin. "Mom will know what to do."

"Oh, no, it's not good, dumbhead. If she and Dad find out about this, they might not let us take care of Ferdie."

"You might have to get a tetanus shot."

"Naw. A little Bactine and a Band-Aid will do. Go down and keep your mom busy while I clean up."

"He might bite you again," said Benjamin.

"Naw. He knows we're even now."

"Benjamin? Casey?" Mollie called out again.

Benjamin opened the door a crack and Ferdie streaked out ahead of him, yapping all the way down the stairs.

Mollie released a bloodcurdling scream. "Help! Help! Jenny, dial 911! There's a wild stray dog in our house!"

I slapped my palm to my cheek and rolled my eyes to the ceiling.

Chapter 6

Word from the Front Office

I convinced Mollie not to call the dogcatcher. But when I tried to explain about Ferdie she cut me off and said we would discuss it when Dad got home. That was just as well. I knew right then Mollie was so hungry from her diet that she would say no to anything that she couldn't stick in her mouth and chew up.

I took Ferdie out to the back-back and promised him a nice red bow to wear over his topknot. He nuzzled my bandaged hand and whimpered a little. I felt a lot better after we had made up. I went back inside and prepared a snack of carrot and celery sticks for Mollie.

When Dad walked in the house he said, "Who belongs to the mangy mutt out in the back-back?"

"We'll discuss it over dinner," said Mollie, placing the food on the table. "Sit down. I'm starving."

We had green salad, green beans, and salmon. The fish had itty-bitty specks of green stuff all over it, as if we didn't already have enough green things to eat. I ate with my left hand and hid my bandaged hand in my lap.

"This time I'm putting my foot down," said Mollie. "That dog has got to go."

"But Mrs. Beasel is in Missoura," I said.

"Missouri," said Benjamin.

"You mean someone dumped that mangy mutt on you kids and skipped town?" asked Dad.

"Ferdie is not a mutt," said Benjamin. "He comes from a long lineage of AKC-registered miniature poodle champions."

Mollie and Dad exchanged looks across the table and burst into laughter.

"I'd say someone sold you kids a bill of goods," said Dad. "But if this Beasel woman really left town, I guess we're stuck with old Ferdie."

"We are not!" exclaimed Mollie. "Casey, you know better than to get a dog without asking our permission; and Jack, you're rewarding her for doing it." She pointed her fork at me. "I put up with dirty socks in your clean-clothes drawer"—she wagged her fork at Benjamin—"and your smelly chemistry experiments"—she hooked an eyebrow at Dad—"and your noisy ball games, but I'm not going to clean up after a dog. Either he goes or I go."

"He *is* going," I said. "In two weeks. We're just taking care of him while Mrs. Beasel is in Missoura."

"Missouri," said Mollie. "Colloquial accents are perfectly acceptable for people native to that particular region. People from Missouri may say Missoura, but we in California say Missouri."

"Missouri," I repeated dutifully.

Mollie gave me a pert little nod. Lecturing always cheers her up. Before she met me she hardly ever got to do any because Benjamin already knows everything.

"Who is this Mrs. Beasel," asked Dad, "and why would she ask you kids to take care of her dog?"

"She's a neighbor lady over on Mendota," I said. "And she didn't exactly ask. We offered."

"Whatever gave you that idea?" asked Mollie.

"Well, we love animals," I said.

"But mainly it's for the capital," said Benjamin.

"Capital!" exclaimed Dad. "You mean you asked this woman to *pay* you?"

"Of course," said Benjamin. "Why else would we go into the pet care business?"

Molly clapped her hands. "Oh my little entrepreneur! His first business venture and he's only ten years old. I'm going to call Mama tonight and tell her all about it."

"Well, tell her it was *my* idea," I nearly shouted. "It's called *Casey Wooster's* Pet Care and Grooming Service."

Mollie tried not to look disappointed, but she's a lousy actress. "That doesn't sound fair."

"I opted to be a silent partner my first time out," said Benjamin. He took a long swig of milk and tried to look as cool as anyone could with a milk mustache. "In case we have to file chapter thirteen."

"Where does he *get* all this stuff?" asked Dad.

Mollie flashed Benjamin her My Amazing Son look and mussed his hair like it wasn't already sticking up. "I hardly think bankruptcy at age ten counts for your permanent financial portfolio, sweetie."

"I don't like this one bit," said Dad. "It's one thing to take in a poor homeless mutt. It's quite another to take on the responsibility of caring for someone else's pet."

I couldn't believe it. Usually when I got Mollie on my side, I was over the hump. This time Dad was the hump parent.

"I think we should let them, Jack," said Mollie. "It's a good lesson in responsibility and the kids need something to do this summer, especially since Casey won't be able to go . . . I mean, considering her mother's sudden change of plans."

Dad thoughtfully stabbed a green bean. "All right then. But check with us before you take on any new clients."

"Well, Dad," I began slowly, "the fact is, we already have." Then I started talking really fast. "The Burrs's two cats. But they're not coming here, we're going there, but only once a day for three days. We start tomorrow."

"You're house-sitting, too?" asked Mollie. "Well, that's different. What if the place burns down? What if you forget to lock up and it gets robbed? What if—"

I halted her with an outstretched palm. "We won't play with matches in their house, we promise. We'll always lock the door when we leave, we promise. If someone breaks in, they'll probably leave before taking anything—the smell will be too much for them."

Mollie muffled a giggle with her hand. She peered over at Dad and said, "You know, she's right."

"We're giving your pet service the Good-Parenting Seal of Approval," said Dad. "Just be responsible."

"Gee, thanks, Dad," I said. I knew I should thank Mollie, too, but I was mad at her for mentioning Mom. I can't stand her to say anything bad about my mom, even if it's true and she says it in a nice way. I know she's really thinking my mom is a terrible mother and she's perfect.

"Just one more thing, Casey," said Mollie. "I don't want you to ever let that dog in this house again."

"But Mrs. Beasel says Ferdie is used to sleeping in her nice, soft, warm bed at night."

"The garage is good enough for Ferdie," said Mollie. "I don't want your beds full of fleas. And no sneaking around at night. Is that clear, Casey?"

"Yes, Mollie," I said.

"Good. Then it's settled."

Phew, I thought.

Chapter 7

Two Difficult Clients

At bedtime we moved Ferdie and his little doll's crib into the garage. He spent the whole night howling and kept everyone awake, except for Benjamin, who sleeps like the living dead. By the time I got up, Dad and Mollie had already gone to work and Jenny was parked on the sofa in front of the TV, the phone glued to her ear. I ate a bowl of cereal, then went outside.

Benjamin was out in the back-back and Ferdie was play-ing fetch with him. Benjamin threw the ball, Ferdie watched it fly through the air, then lay down and put his chin on his paws. After a while, Benjamin fetched.

"Did Mollie and Dad complain about all the howling?" I asked.

"They weren't thrilled about it," said Benjamin. "Mom

could hardly roll out of bed and Dad sleepwalked through breakfast."

I sank to the grass and patted Ferdie's moussed topknot. "You were homesick for Mrs. Beasel's soft, warm bed, weren't you? You'll do better tonight, won't you, boy?"

We got Ferdie's leash and took him on a walk around the circle. Bradley Singer was out on his skateboard. It was strange to see him in the light of day. He looks a little like the Pillsbury Doughboy, all white and pasty. He's a Nintendo nut, always bragging about getting about a million on Mario. Once he put a joystick into Benjamin's hand and Benj didn't know what end was up. Bradley had a good laugh over that one. Tiffany Levitsky, a little first grader with long yellow braids who lives next door to Bradley, was outside, too. She had put a kickboard on top of a skate and was trying to imitate Bradley's skateboarding.

"Bug off," he told her.

"Be nice or I'm telling my mother," said Tiffany.

Bradley grazed her kickboard with his ankle, causing it to slide off the skate. "Oops, sorry," he said. He noticed us and called. "Your parents aren't really letting you have a pet care service." He must have read one of our fliers.

"Here's one of our clients," said Benjamin. He held up the handle of Ferdie's leash.

"*Cli-ent!*" mocked Bradley. "Look at that ridiculous-looking mutt. Wait here, I'll go get my goldfish."

I stopped walking, but Benjamin kept going, his shoulders slumped and a scowl on his face.

"Hey, I said hold up," Bradley called after him. "I can give you ten days of business. We're going to Disney World—

not dumb old Disneyland, Disney World in Florida. I bet you've never been there."

"We don't take goldfish," said Benjamin.

Bradley ignored him and ran into his house.

"What do you mean, we don't take goldfish?" I asked.

"Goldfish are tricky. In other words, they die. Our luck Bradley's would die and I'd never hear the end of it."

Tiffany reached out to pet Ferdie. He bared his teeth and let out a low growl. I stepped between them. "Careful, now, he's a little shy around strangers."

Tiffany puffed out her lower lip. "I'm telling my mom your dog tried to bite me."

"He's not ours. We're just taking care of him."

"Could you take care of my pony?" asked Tiffany.

"No," said Benjamin. "Too big."

"Sure, we could," I said. I couldn't believe such luck! "You have a pony? I didn't know you had a pony!"

"I'll go get him." Tiffany ran toward her house.

Bradley came out of his house holding a fishbowl where his head should have been. He ran down the driveway slopping water all over the place. I got a glimpse of Bradley's eyeballs swimming around behind glass, then a wave of cold water crushed against my chest. I sucked in my breath and noticed I was now holding the goldfish bowl. Inside was a little fish colored blue, purple, brown, yellow, red, orange, and black.

"Hey, this goldfish isn't gold," I said.

"It's a Bristol Shubunkin," said Bradley. "They're very rare."

"They're feeders," said Benjamin. "They go for a dime a

piece. It's not economically feasible to pay three dollars a day—thirty bucks in all—to have us take care of it."

Bradley put his hands on his hips and bent his face down close to Benjamin's. "Are you saying I can't afford it?"

We knew he could afford anything he wanted: real Rollerblades and shoes you pump air into and collector's baseball cards. I once overheard Dad telling Mollie that Bradley's parents must have about twenty credit cards charged up to the limit. I figured if he wanted to throw away his parents' money he might as well toss some in our direction. "You can't put a price on the head of a loving, warm, cuddly pet," I told Benjamin. I glanced down at the goldfish and added, "Or even a loving, wet, slimy one." I looked at Bradley and said, "Sorry, but we don't accept American Express."

"Come on, Oats, come on, girl," Tiffany called. She was leading, or rather dragging, her pony over the sidewalk. One look at it and my heart sank down to my ankles. Its body was made out of an oatmeal box. There were popsicle sticks for legs, thread spools for feet, and yarn for the mane and tail. It was pretty cute, but not nearly as good as a real pony.

"Oh, no. We're not taking that thing," said Benjamin.

"You're taking Bradley's goldfish," said Tiffany. "I'm telling my mother you don't play fair."

"We're not playing," said Benjamin. "We're running a real business and we don't take oatmeal boxes."

"I'm telling you called Oats names," said Tiffany.

"I suppose you can't afford three dollars a day," I said to Tiffany.

"Isn't that kind of high for you guys? How 'bout a nickel?"

"Fine," I said. "Let's take our new customers home, Benj."

Tiffany held out her string reins to Benjamin. Bradley let out a belly laugh and Benjamin's ears turned magenta. He glared at me. "I'm not dragging that thing around."

"I've got my hands full." I pleaded to Benjamin with my eyes and lowered my voice. "Pick it up and let's go."

Benjamin tucked Oats under his arm and Bradley laughed again. "Don't forget to brush him down tonight, True."

Benjamin jerked on Ferdie's leash and started walking fast. I tried to catch up to him and another bone-chilling tidal wave hit my chest. "Hey, wait up."

Benjamin stopped and turned. "Have you no integrity? Why get involved with the little tattletale?"

"It just seemed easier to let her have her way."

"We don't even know how long we're stuck with this thing."

"Who cares? I'll just stash old Oats somewhere safe until Tiffany's family comes home from vacation."

"All right, but from now on I'm screening our clients. If this fish goes belly-up, Bradley will make sure I do, too."

When we got home, I set Oats on the top shelf of my hutch, next to my horse statue collection. After lunch Benjamin made me go to the library with him and lug home a ton of books about goldfish care. He spent the rest of the afternoon with his nose either stuck in one of the books or pressed up against the goldfish bowl.

"Aha!" he cried out. "See there! The first signs of Ichthyophthirius. See that spot? Do you remember if it had this spot this morning?"

I studied the fish. "Which spot? He's got a million of them and they're all different colors. He's pretty, don't you think? Did you catch his name?"

"It's probably Terminal. Bradley stuck me with a diseased fish so it will die and he can pound me for it."

"Quit worrying, will ya? How about a round of Monopoly?"

"Only if I'm banker."

Finally I got Benjamin interested in something besides fish death. When Dad and Mollie got home from work, they gave us the okay on our new customers. They both had a good laugh over Oats, which made Benjamin's ears turn magenta again.

After dinner Benjamin and I walked down to the Burrs's. It was still plenty light out. Their house didn't look scary at all, especially since we knew creepy old Wilbur Burr wasn't around to jump out at us. We unlocked the back door, fed the cats, changed their water, and used the pooper-scooper. The whole operation took about five minutes.

We were just about to lock up again when Benjamin said, "Hey, we still haven't seen the cats."

"I'm sure they're fine. Let's go."

Benjamin walked into the living room. "Here, Spook! Here, Boo!" he called out.

"Remember, Mrs. Burr said they don't like strangers."

"Let's check the bedrooms," said Benjamin.

He started down the hall and I followed. One door was shut. It had a little kid's license plate nailed to it that read WILBUR. On a piece of binder paper was scrawled in big letters: KEEP OUT, WOOSTER BRATS.

"Maybe they got shut in here in Wilbur's bedroom," I said. I placed my hand on the knob.

"Hold it!" exclaimed Benjamin. "If Wilbur says keep out, we better keep out. He's probably got some booby trap rigged up. We open the door and a whole can of paint douses us."

"Oh pooh, you're overestimating him." But I turned and walked toward the back door anyway. No use pushing our luck.

We locked up and walked home.

When we stepped into the kitchen, Mollie said, "Bradley and his mother were by while you were gone. They dropped off these. I didn't know you two know how to care for plants."

On the table were two big cardboard boxes loaded with them. Another box contained all sorts of supplies: plant food, plant cleaner, spray bottles, potting soil, a little shovel, and a note from Bradley:

You didn't really think we were going to pay you three bucks a day for taking care of one stinking little goldfish, did you? P.S. You better take good care of my mom's plants. We're not paying for no dead ones.

I raised my eyebrows at Mollie.

"Don't look at me, sweetie. This here is a black thumb." She stuck her thumb up to show me, but it looked as pale as the rest of her.

"I sure hope you guys know what you're doing," said Dad.

"We don't," said Benjamin, "but we're going to find out."

I groaned. That meant another backbreaking trip home from the library, followed by hours and hours of study. I left

Benjamin to sort through the box of plant supplies while I went out to get Ferdie settled down for the night. I led him into the garage and patted the doll mattress. Ferdie refused to lie on it. He sniffed the cold cement.

"I know you don't like it out here, but I can't do a thing about it. Can't you just make the best of it?"

Ferdie stepped reluctantly onto the doll mattress. He turned around twice, stopped, headed in the other direction, then collapsed, midcircle, as if he were too tired to make it all the way around. He gazed up at me, his eyes looking like two melted chocolate chips.

I almost melted myself. It took all my willpower to turn my back on him and head for the kitchen door. I looked over my shoulder at Ferdie one last time. He whimpered.

"You'll be okay. Just keep it down tonight, will you please?" I switched off the light and hurried inside.

Chapter 8

The Science of the Future

At least Ferdie didn't howl *all* night. He quieted down around 3:00 A.M. Benjamin had already eaten breakfast by the time I got up. He went to let Ferdie out of the garage while I ate a bowl of cereal.

Dad stumbled into the kitchen. His eyes were set deep into dark sockets. He poured his coffee too long and the mug overflowed onto the counter. While cleaning that up, he knocked the sugar bowl over. The sugar drifted to the floor like snow. I jumped up and got the broom and dustpan and started sweeping up.

"Two sleepless nights is the limit for me, Casey," said Dad. "That mutt keeps me awake another night it's off to the kennel."

"The kennel! That would cost a lot more than what Mrs. Beasel is paying us."

"So you and Benjamin won't have an allowance for half a year. At least I'll get some sleep."

Mollie stalked into the kitchen, dressed for work, holding my ripped jeans.

"You snooped!" I exclaimed. "You pawed through my private stuff!" I had Dad and Mom's wedding picture stashed away in my top dresser drawer and I was embarrassed to think Mollie might have found it.

"If I didn't go looking for your dirty clothes once in a while the health department would come shut us down." She held out the jeans. "These were brand new. What happened to them?"

"Well, uh, it takes Ferdie a little while to warm up to strangers and—"

"Uh-huh," said Mollie, "that dog again. The very same dog, I suppose, that bit your hand!"

I flung my hand behind my back. I forgot the bandage had come off in my bathwater the night before.

"Bite! Let me see that!" Dad covered the distance between us in one giant step.

"It's nothing," I said. "The skin is barely broken."

"I hope that vicious mutt has had all his shots."

"Ferdie isn't vicious—just scared. We tried to groom him like a poodle, and he sort of panicked."

Dad held my hand and examined the bite carefully from all sides. "You better call Dr. Dodd when you get to the office, Mollie. See if he can work Casey in for a tetanus shot late this afternoon."

"*Your* daughter brought that dog into this house, you call the doctor," said Mollie.

"I'm sure *your* son had something to do with it."

This was bad news. Usually Benjamin and I belonged to both of them.

Mollie tossed the jeans on the counter and grabbed her briefcase. "Have a nice day," she said to Dad and me in a not-very-nice tone. She shut the back door soundly behind her.

I had never seen Mollie leave the house without kissing Dad good-bye. I had always wished they would start fighting with each other, so Dad would divorce her and remarry Mom. But now that I had actually seen them fight I felt just terrible. What if Dad didn't remarry Mom? What if he married another lady and I got an even worse stepmother? What if I never got to see Mollie and Benjamin again? Ferdie was tearing our family apart.

The doorbell rang.

"There's Jenny," said Dad. "Do me a favor, Case, and don't take on a tarantula or rattlesnake today."

"I'll try not to, Daddy." I kissed him good-bye.

I said hello to Jenny, then dashed out back. Benjamin was sitting on the patio swing. He was staring out into the yard, his face turned away from me.

I plopped down next to him. "The front office knows about my pants, my bite—everything. Boy, am I in trouble now, and it's all because of that stupid dog. I don't know how I can stand him another twelve days."

"You won't have to," said Benjamin. "He's gone."

"Oh, no! How'd he get out?" I jumped up. "Come on, get the leash. We gotta go look for him."

Benjamin turned to me. Tears were running down his

chubby cheeks. His face was about as pale as his hair. He rubbed one hand over the other. "Not that kind of gone. I mean long gone. Ferdie is dead."

"Ferdie dead? No way." I couldn't believe it, I wouldn't. I couldn't just crumple up inside and get all shaky and teary-eyed. I imagined Ferdie in a deep sleep, and when he saw me, his head would pop up to greet me.

I walked toward the garage, taking big steps, my shoulders back. I tried to look brave for Benjamin's sake, but my heart was thumping fast and hard. I broke into a run and flung open the garage door. Ferdie was still out of sight, behind some boxes. I stopped and called out, "Ferdie." My voice cracked. I called louder. "Here, boy, breakfast time." I puckered my lips and blew air through them, but no whistle came out.

It was quiet in the garage. Too quiet.

I felt Benjamin's jagged breathing at my shoulder. "I told you," he said.

We walked past the stack of boxes and around the boat. There was Ferdie, curled up on the doll mattress. His chin was resting on his haunches. His eyes were closed. He looked just like he was asleep, except he was too still. His side wasn't moving up and down. I squatted down beside him and I put my hand in front of his nose, trying to feel his breath. Nothing.

I had never touched a dead thing, and I didn't want to now, but I had to do what I could for Ferdie. I curled my fingers into a fist and slugged him in the chest.

"Ahhh!" Benjamin screamed, high-pitched and shrill.

"Shut up!" I hit Ferdie again, then again.

Benjamin grabbed my raised fist. I tried to shake him off, but his fear made him stronger than usual. "Stop that! It's sick."

"You stop, I'm trying to save him!" I wrenched my hand free and slugged Ferdie's heart again, trying to jolt it back to work.

"Oh," said Benjamin. "Cardiopulmonary resuscitation. I thought you had gone stark raving mad."

Ferdie was just as still as before. I put my face down next to his and tried to pry his teeth open with my thumbs.

"Casey! Stop! You aren't really going to put your mouth on dead dog lips, are you?"

"How else am I going to give him artificial respiration?"

"That's not going to work any more than the CPR. Ferdie has been dead too long. He's already stiff."

I sat up. I was relieved I wouldn't have to touch my lips with dead dog lips, but I would have done it to save Ferdie. I looked around the garage, trying to think what else we could do. I spotted the fuse box, walked over to it, and opened it up.

"Hey, Benj, we can hook Ferdie up to this somehow. We'll pull this lever and send electricity through his body— then *pow*—he'll come alive just like Frankenstein's monster."

Benjamin slapped his brow. "Frankenstein is a made-up story."

"No, it's not. I saw it in an old, old movie."

"So what? It's still fiction."

I was about eight when I saw *Frankenstein*. It really scared the bejabbers out of me because I thought the movie was so old that special effects hadn't been invented yet, and they could only make movies of things that really happened. I had gone on believing that without giving it much thought until now, when I was old enough to know better.

The inside of my skin turned prickly and my blood pounded in my ears. Benjamin got warped into a diagonal in my blurry vision. "We can't just let Ferdie *die*."

"I don't think he needs our permission."

I walked over and sat on the cool cement floor next to Ferdie. "This can't be happening." I had this hard guilty feeling pushing against the inside of my chest. I wanted to keep it hidden there and not tell Benjamin. Maybe if I didn't talk about it, it would just go away. I let out a long, heavy sigh, but my bad feelings didn't escape with all that air. Instead, the pressure built up more and more until I just had to spill my guts. "I killed Ferdie," I whispered.

"You?" Benjamin sat down next to me. "How do you mean?"

"I fed him all those doggie treats on the way home."

"Mrs. Beasel overfed him all the time."

"I upset him real bad trying to groom him."

"He probably liked the attention," said Benjamin.

"And maybe not. Mrs. Beasel said he wasn't used to it anymore. He probably died of shock."

"Ah no," said Benjamin. "You probably poisoned him when he bit you."

I raised my fist to slug him. He folded his arms over his

head and laughed. His laugh startled me. I know you aren't supposed to laugh when someone dies, and yet I snickered, too.

"I was only trying to get you to stop blaming yourself," he said. "Remember, Mrs. Beasel said Ferdie was real old. He had a good, long life. He died of natural causes."

The pressure seeped out of my chest like air out of a balloon. I didn't feel guilty anymore. Guilt was replaced by sadness, like I could only feel one real bad feeling at a time. "Oh, I wish we never started this dumb pet care service. What will we tell Mrs. Beasel? Ferdie was all she had. He was her companion in life."

"She'll probably scream and yell at us," said Benjamin.

"Crying is worse," I said. "I just hate it when grown-ups cry. It's so scary. When my mom first ran away, sometimes she'd call me up just to cry. Half of that big telephone bill of hers is just tears. I sure hope Mrs. Beasel doesn't do that much crying. What if she faints? She's too heavy for us to catch her."

"She could have a heart attack or something," said Benjamin.

"Oh, oh, I miss my mom," I said. "I wish she was here right now. We could tell her about this and she would help us through it." Anger seeped into my voice. "She wouldn't go make us 'accept our responsibility' like Dad and Mollie."

I expected an argument from Benjamin, but he kept quiet. He stood up and unhooked the shovel from the wall.

I jumped up. "What are you doing?"

"We have to bury Ferdie. In the back-back."

"We can't do that. Mrs. Beasel will want to see him one last time. She'll want to say good-bye."

"Well, we can't save him for twelve days. He'll decompose."

"Not if we put him in the deep freeze."

"Oh, no," said Benjamin. "He'll contaminate our food."

"Not if we wrap him up real good. He'll be as harmless as an old popsicle."

"A fur-covered popsicle? The front office would never go for it."

"They'll never know. The freezer is huge. Ferdie is small. He'd be easy to hide."

"Maybe," said Benjamin. "Let me think about this." He rested his shoulder against the shovel handle and stared down at the cement. "Hey, you know about . . . oh, never mind, you're the wrong person to tell."

I put my hands on my hips, bent forward, and nearly shouted, "What? I'm the wrong person to tell *what?*"

"About cryonics—the science of the future. It's in that book I'm reading about cryogenics. There are a lot of dead guys hanging around in freezers waiting for scientists to figure out a way to bring them back to life."

"You're putting me on," I said. "That's more far out than Frankenstein's monster."

"But it's true. Walt Disney wanted to do that, but when he died his family wouldn't go for it."

"Then it's our *duty* to freeze Ferdie. I sure hope the science of the future gets here fast—like in a little under twelve days." I walked over to the deep freeze, a large rectangular chest that hits me waist high. I pulled the latch and lifted the top. It sprang up out of my reach. I pulled out a couple of packages of frozen vegetables.

"Wait," said Benjamin. "Let's get Ferdie ready first."

I dropped the food back into the freezer. I had to jump up a couple times before I could reach the top. I pulled it shut and latched it.

Both Benjamin and I squatted down over Ferdie. I ran my hand over him, from his mousse-stiffened topknot to his straggly tail. His fur felt the same as usual, but underneath it he was cold and stiff.

"Good-bye, Ferdie," Benjamin said sadly.

I put my faith in the science of the future and said, "See you later, old boy."

We wrapped him in the doll blanket, then put him in a big plastic garbage bag. Benjamin twisted the wire tie about twenty times. I guess he was still worried about dead dog cooties getting out on our food. I opened the freezer again and began handing food out to Benjamin. He put it down on the cement floor. There was a lot of stuff in the freezer. It took us a long time to haul it out.

"There's already a dead animal in here," I said. "A whole cow. Look at all this steak and hamburger. I wish we could have a barbecue tonight. With hamburgers and potato salad and s'mores for dessert."

"None of that is on my mom's diet," said Benjamin.

"I'm sick of your mom's diet. If I eat another fish, I'll grow scales and fins." I bent down into the freezer again. At first it felt good to stick my head into a freezer on a hot summer morning, but now I was getting a headache. My hands were so numb I could hardly hold on to the frozen packages. The hole I was digging in the food was getting pretty big. I had to jump up onto the side of the freezer and balance on my tummy, my feet dangling about a foot off the floor. I reached a little too far and slid into the freezer head first. Benjamin grabbed a leg and pulled me out. I hopped to the floor to take a breather.

"This food is starting to defrost and Jenny may come looking for us any minute," said Benjamin. "What's left way down there, anyway?"

I peered into the deep freeze. "Just an old box of Christmas candy, that yucky kind with the soft centers. Probably everyone has forgotten about it."

"My mom never forgets about chocolate."

"She'd never cheat on her diet. She's too perfect."

"She isn't perfect. Who said she is?"

"Well, she sure *acts* like she is."

"She does not!"

I held up my palms. "Okay, no time to argue now."

Together we picked up Ferdie and lowered him into the freezer as gently as we could. We had to let go right at the end and he sort of smashed the box of candy. Then we both tossed food in as fast as we could. Toward the top we went a little slower and stacked it up neater.

I jumped up and grabbed the handle of the freezer top. Just before shutting it, I slipped a package of hamburger out. "I'm going to pretend I accidentally left this out," I said. "By the time Dad and Mollie get home, it will be defrosted. Dad will barbecue it rather than throw it out."

"Very tricky," said Benjamin. "You think he might wonder what we were accidentally doing in the freezer?"

"Oh, shoot!" I opened the freezer, tossed the hamburger back in, and slammed it shut.

Chapter 9

Mollie and I Have a Fight

Benjamin and I spent the rest of the day doing house plant research. First we had to identify all the plants by matching them with pictures in some huge library books. We figured out that the one with little leaves growing out of big leaves was a piggyback and the one with skinny leaves in the shape of a Dr. Seuss hairdo was a spider plant. Philodendron looked like someone had cut big chunks out of its floppy, shiny leaves and spotted laurel looked like it had been splatter-painted with light green. There were three kinds of African violets. The one with blue flowers was Sailor Girl, the purple one was Ruffled Queen, and the white one was Snow Prince.

"Uh-oh," I said. "According to this book if you got African violets, you got trouble. It has a whole list of don'ts here. Don't keep plants in direct sunlight, don't get water on the leaves, don't let the soil get soggy, don't allow the stems to touch the rim of the pot, and don't forget to feed it regularly."

"Does it say anything you *do?*" Benjamin asked.

I pretended to read, "Cross your fingers and hope they don't die."

"It doesn't say that. Give it here." Benjamin snatched the book from me and began reading. He turned the page and pointed at a picture. "Hey, here's a Venus's-flytrap. It says it has the ability to catch and digest its prey."

"Cool!" I leaned over to have a look. "Do we have one?"

"Nope. Remember, the Singers took Bradley with them."

We had a good laugh over that one.

"This plant here looks like Rabbit Tracks Maranta," I said. "What a cute name. Those dark green spots do look like rabbit tracks. The book doesn't say anything about these brown spots though."

"What brown spots?" Benjamin bent to examine the plant. "I don't believe it! They dumped an unhealthy plant on us! Quick, look up what causes the brown spots."

"It's right here. Too much watering."

"So we'll let up on the water for a while." Benjamin pointed to a short spiky plant. "This is an aloe vera. It says it can heal minor burns and insect bites."

"No kidding."

"Yeah. You just cut off a leaf, squeeze its juice out, and bandage the leaf onto your burn."

I held out my hand. "Try it on where Ferdie bit me."

Benjamin got out the first-aid kit. He applied the aloe

vera to my hand and bandaged it up. "Well, how does it feel?"

"Fine."

"A miracle cure!" exclaimed Benjamin.

"It felt okay before." The big spiky leaf sticking out of both ends of the Band-Aid made my hand look pretty stupid.

About that time Dad came home. He laughed and said, "Hey, Case, why do you have that leaf strapped onto your hand?"

"Miracle cure," Benjamin explained.

While Dad drove me to the doctor's office I got more and more depressed thinking about Ferdie in the freezer. When Dr. Dodd stuck the needle in my bottom I didn't even cry. I figured I deserved it since Ferdie had died. Then I got to thinking about taping some aloe vera to my bottom and that made me smile to myself.

At dinner I had to balance on one side of my bottom, because the other side was too sore to sit on. I put a forkful of fillet of sole in my mouth and almost gagged. I couldn't even stand the smell of it. I put my napkin up to my mouth and pretended to cough. With my tongue, I pushed the fish out of my mouth into the napkin. I placed the napkin in my lap. I worked the plastic cap off one of the hollow aluminum legs of our kitchen table. I unwrapped the piece of fish and shoved it down into the table leg.

Over the years, I've filled these table legs with a lot of yucky food: lima beans, broccoli, bread pudding, and now fish. I keep expecting to fill the whole thing up, but I haven't yet. I wonder what happens to the stuff. Maybe it dries up.

Maybe mice eat it. Maybe someone cleans it out without mentioning it to me.

"Casey!" Mollie said sharply, pointing her fork at me. "Next week when I do laundry, I want to see not four, not six, but *seven* pairs of dirty little girls' underwear."

I groaned and slid down in my chair until my chin about hit the table. Benjamin threw back his head and hooted up at the ceiling like a wolf howling at the moon.

"Change every day, Casey," said Mollie. "Every morning put on a nice, clean, fresh pair of—"

"I get the message!" I snapped.

Mollie raised her eyebrows at Dad and held up two fingers.

Dad grinned and shook his head. Benjamin hooted again. I blew hot air up into my bangs. "Can we just *drop* it?" I yelled at Mollie.

Her gray eyes got big. "What?" she asked innocently.

Boy, that really toasted me. Like I was too dumb to know she was still on the same subject.

Mollie took a tiny bite of fish, she chewed it about twenty times, then took a sip of water. "Hmmm, dinner tastes so much better when I don't snack between meals. I've been absolutely perfect on my diet for two whole weeks."

"Two whole weeks?" repeated Dad. "And not one sweet roll off the snack cart during coffee break?"

"That's right," said Mollie, proudly.

"Not one little candy bar on your afternoon break?"

Mollie shook her head. "Not one." She scraped her plate and licked her fork.

"Not even an itsy-bitsy little hot fudge sundae at the lunch counter with the girls?"

"I resent that!" Mollie glared at Dad.

He gave her a surprised look back. While they were so busy gawking at each other I slipped some more fish down the hollow table leg.

"Calm down, sweetie," said Dad. "You've been trying to lose the same ten pounds ever since the day I met you. And every time you launch into one of these diets you swear you aren't cheating. Can I help it if I'm a little suspicious?"

"Can I help it if a man's metabolism is a zillion times faster than a woman's?" exclaimed Mollie. "Can I help it if I gain a pound by inhaling a whiff of chocolate cake?" She shot up from the table and slung her purse over her shoulder. "And since I'm so *weak* and need to avoid *all temptation* I better get out of the kitchen right away. Come on, Casey, we girls are going shopping."

I hate it when Mollie says "we girls," meaning her and me. I groaned and slid down in my seat again. It gave me an opportunity to make another deposit. "Do I have to?"

"We have to replace those jeans that dog destroyed."

"Oh! How is old Ferdie?" asked Dad. "Gee, he's been so quiet I forgot all about him." He yawned and stretched. "He better not be saving up to howl his head off all night."

Benjamin gave me a nervous look.

"I'm full," I said quickly, shoving my plate away. Actually the table leg was full.

The mall was much more tempting for Mollie than fish leftovers in our own kitchen. When we passed the bakery she raised her chin and wiggled her nose like a kitty catching a whiff of a smelly garbage can. We passed Farley's Ice Cream Parlor and she stared at the giant poster of a gooey banana split like it was some dreamy movie star. In front of the Nut Hut she ground to a halt and went into a sort of trance.

Finally we made it to Naylor's Department Store. Just my luck—they were having a preseason sale. There ought to be a law against selling scratchy wool clothes in the middle of summer.

Mollie picked out about a hundred things for her and me to try on. Worst of all, she made me share a dressing room with her. She took off her blouse and skirt right in front of me. Her skin was about as white as her underwear. She had this little roll of flab that rose over the top of her panties like an uncooked doughnut. She tugged on a pair of pants that were so tight I thought the zipper would bust open. She turned and looked over her shoulder. All three of her reflections frowned back at her.

She had to wiggle her bottom real hard to get the pants off. "These will fit just perfectly after those last five pounds come off," she said cheerfully. She held up an icky dress with a sailor's collar on it. "Now your turn, Casey."

"I hate dresses."

"Ah, come on. Let's just see how it looks."

"Oh, all right." I pulled my T-shirt over my head.

Mollie was gawking at my chest. "Oh my, Casey! You're budding!"

I slapped my arms across my chest. "What do you think I am, a rosebush?"

"Maybe we should try some training bras."

"Who ever thought up that dumb name? What are they in training *for*? Mine are still so flat the bra would slip up around my neck and strangle me."

Mollie sighed. "Perhaps it is a bit premature." She put the ugly dress over my head and pulled it down. One minute she wants to buy me a bra and the next minute she's dressing me like I'm a baby. She looked at me in the mirror. "Oh, you look adorable."

"It stinks. Don't buy it. I won't wear it, not ever."

"We'll see about that," said Mollie.

She tried on a bunch of other stuff. She made me put on six pairs of jeans when the first pair fit just fine. Then we had to wait in a big, long line. We were going to get home so late, I wouldn't be able to watch any TV. I had been so busy with houseplants I hadn't gotten to play all day. I was hungry and a little sorry I had fed my dinner to the table. I thought about Ferdie in our freezer. My bottom started to itch. The scratchy wool dress had irritated it.

Finally we got up to the cash register. The sales clerk held up the icky sailor dress. "How sweet!"

Mollie grinned. "And it looks so cute on my daughter."

"I am *not* your daughter and you are not my mom! My mom would never make me wear clothes I hate and she would never make me eat fish three nights a week." The angry words rushed out of my mouth before I thought through them.

Mollie's mouth formed an O. The sales clerk and the people in line stared at me. I turned and ran out of the store.

Out on the mall, I found a bench. I sat down hard and

hurt my bottom. I waited for what seemed like hours. Finally Mollie walked out of the store lugging her packages. She looked like someone getting off a plane who can't find the person who is supposed to meet her. She spotted me and her worried look melted into a smile. She walked over to me.

"There you are." She took her foot out of her high heel, scrunched up her toes, then stretched them out. "Ah! That line was so long, I thought I'd never get out of there." She slipped her shoe back on. "Let's take a break."

We went back to Farley's Ice Cream Parlor and Mollie let me have anything I wanted. I ordered a double-scooped Chocolate Suicide: chocolate chocolate chip ice cream, hot fudge, hot caramel, chocolate-flavored marshmallow cream, extra whipped cream, and chocolate sprinkles on top.

"And what about you, ma'am?" the waitress asked Mollie.

"Oh . . . just water. I'm dieting."

"Our frozen yogurt has only eighty calories per scoop."

"Ah . . . no, thanks." Mollie's no sounded like yes.

My sundae was really yummy, but I felt just awful eating it in front of Mollie. Her mouth opened every bite I took.

"My mom never diets and she's thin," I said.

Mollie's eyes got wide. "Never? Well, some of us girls have to work a little harder to look good." Mollie could work *real* hard and *never* look as good as my mom, and she probably knew it. She met my mom last year during bathing suit weather.

"Mom *used* to diet. But she says when she stopped dieting she stopped having a weight problem. The more she deprived herself, the more good things she craved. She ate a whole lot more by blowing her diet than eating normally."

"*Some* people just have no willpower. Oh, Casey, you're dripping hot fudge." Mollie swiped her finger across my chin, then thoughtfully licked it. After a moment she said, "You know, you weren't very nice to me in Naylor's."

"Sorry," I said. "I was in a bad mood."

"I didn't buy that dress. It was wrong of me to inflict my tastes on you."

"*And* it was wrong of you to talk about my dirty underwear at the dinner table in front of Benjamin."

"Honestly, Casey, he's your stepbrother."

"He's also a boy in my class. And I hated it when you stared at my chest. I'm not going to need a bra for years."

Mollie smiled, cocked her head, and touched her earring. "That's funny. When I was a girl, I couldn't wait until—"

"You and I are different in case you haven't noticed."

"I've noticed, Casey. Can't we get along anyway? I am married to your dad. That does make me your stepmother. What you said in the store hurt me deeply."

I puffed some air up at my bangs. I was sorry about that, but sometimes kids have to hurt grown-ups to get their point across. "You're my dad's wife and my friend's mother, but to me you're just Mollie."

"*Just* Mollie?"

"I don't mean it like that. But I already have a mom and one is enough. No one can take her place."

"I clean for you and I cook for you. I take care of you and I take you shopping. That ought to count for something."

"Shopping counts against you. I *hate* shopping. Unless it's with my mom. *She* lets me get what I like."

"Well, I haven't seen her around lately, have you? She can't even be bothered with you in the summer."

"That isn't true!" I nearly shouted back. "She can't afford me." I guess sometimes grown-ups have to hurt kids to get their point across, too. I couldn't take another bite of my Chocolate Suicide sundae. I couldn't even look at it.

Mollie blinked really fast a bunch of times. She pressed her lips together so tight white bumps rose up around them, like she was trying to hold in other mean things she wanted to say about my mom. After a while she took a sip of water, then spoke calmly. "The mother of your friend, huh? So you and Benjamin are friends now?"

I forgot I had said that. It was something I just realized for myself. "We've been through a lot together."

"I guess! All those houseplants! And no telling what that horrible little dog will do next."

I rolled my eyes away from her. "Not much, I have a feeling."

Chapter 10

Spooky and Boo, the Invisible Cats

It was 9:30 by the time Mollie and I got home from shopping. Dad and Benjamin were already cutting the z's. I got ready for bed, but I wasn't sleepy. Too many thoughts were going around in my head. I lay on my bed and wrote:

Dear Mom,

This was the worst day of my life. Ferdie died and Benjamin and I had to hide him in the freezer so Mrs. Beasel can say good-bye to him. I guess you don't know who Ferdie is. Well, I started a pet care and grooming service to raise money to come visit you.

And tonight I had a fight with Mollie. She said you can't

be bothered having me this summer. Is that true? You just don't want me around?

Your brokenhearted daughter,
Casey Wooster

I ripped the letter up, then wrote:

Dear Mom,

How are you doing? Benjamin and I started a pet care and grooming service just for fun. One of our customers is a dog named Ferdie, but he's not feeling that well.

Mollie is on a diet and she is very crabby. She makes us eat fish for breakfast, lunch, and dinner. You are a lot more fun and you are a lot prettier, too.

Love,
Casey Wooster

I turned out the light and got into bed, but I still had a lot of thinking to do. I remembered that before Dad met Mollie we had take-out food all the time and things were always a mess. I didn't mind that much at all. The awful part was how empty and quiet the house was. I had to admit that it's a lot more fun living with Mollie and Benjamin.

Another thought made me bolt upright in bed. The Burrs's cats! I had forgotten all about them! I slipped out of bed and tiptoed out into the hall, making my way by the streetlight shining through my window. I listened for Dad's snoring and Mollie's even breathing. I sneaked into Benjamin's room and tried to shake him awake. He groaned in his sleep and rolled over. I sat on him.

"Hey!" he cried out. "What's the big—"

I covered his mouth and slid to the side of him. "The Burrs's cats," I whispered. "Did you remember to feed them?" I took my hand away from his mouth.

Benjamin shook his head. "We can wait until morning."

"No, we can't. Their little tummies are growling with hunger right now. And what if they yowl their heads off and some neighbor calls the cops? Then we'd—"

"Okay, okay." Benjamin struggled to a seated position. "You go tell Mom and Dad while I get dressed."

"They'd be mad if we woke them up. We'll leave a note."

"When Ferdie hears us up, he'll howl and wake them up anyway."

"Ferdie's dead," I reminded him.

"Oh. I thought it was just part of a bad dream."

"Get dressed. I'll be downstairs."

I wrote the note and left it under the salt shaker on the table. I got out two flashlights and the keys to the Burrs's house. Benjamin stumbled downstairs, dressed and wearing his old glasses with the duct tape over the nosepiece.

We stepped out the back door and passed through the gate. The night air was warm and sticky. Everything was still; not even a car passed. We started running down Barrett Circle, casting long skinny shadows beneath the streetlamps. My skin tingled with the reckless freedom of being out after dark without our parents knowing.

Mendota Way, with no streetlamps, was dark and scary. When we stepped onto the Burrs's walkway a floodlight shot on, causing us to jump into each other's arms. We ducked around the side of the house and unlocked the back door.

I stuck my hand inside and groped for the kitchen light switch, imagining Wilbur Burr on the other side of the door with a meat cleaver raised over his head. Just as I expected my hand to get hacked off, light flooded into the safe, empty kitchen. We stepped inside and shut the door.

"We're crazy, know that?" said Benjamin. "Suppose someone saw us and called the cops?"

"We got a right to be here. Just get on the other end of that pooper-scooper so we can vamoose." I opened the refrigerator and took out the opened can of cat food from yesterday. I scraped the food into one dish, then filled the other one with fresh water. "We still haven't seen these cats."

"Tough. We'll see them tomorrow," said Benjamin. He finished up and moved to the sink to wash up.

I set the water dish down. "I hope they're all right." I took a few steps into the dark living room to see if I could hear the cats prowling around.

"Boooooo! Spoooooky!" Benjamin wailed from the kitchen.

A shiver ran down my spine. I hightailed it across the dark living room and switched on the hall light. I stood at Wilbur's bedroom door, my hand on the knob.

"Don't you dare." Benjamin's voice was suddenly so close behind me that the hairs stood up beneath my ponytail.

"The cats could be trapped in there starving to death."

"Almost anything could be trapped in there," Benjamin

said. "Maybe the smell of this house comes from all the dead bodies Wilbur's got stuffed in his closet."

Wilbur with the meat cleaver sprang into my mind. I gasped and pressed my palm against my chest. My heart was jumping all over the place. "Naw, his mom would never let him keep dead bodies." I took a deep breath and pushed open the door.

"Yikes!" Benjamin ran down the hall.

I flicked on the light and blinked. Every inch of wall space was covered with shelves holding model trains. A pennant from Rio Americano High was tacked to the closet door. The twin-size bed was made up kind of rumply, the way kids do it. On top was a threadbare Davy Crockett bedspread.

"Benj," I called down the hall, "the coast is clear." I got down on my hands and knees and peered under the bed. Nothing but dust bunnies.

"Hey, this looks like a little boy's room," said Benjamin from the door.

"Tell me about it." I peered under the chest of drawers and desk. "The cats aren't in here."

"Did you check the closet?"

"The door is shut. No way they could get in." I wasn't about to come face-to-face with Wilbur Burr's dirty socks . . . or whatever else he kept in there.

Benjamin didn't argue. We turned off the light and shut the door. As we walked down the hall, I heard a scratching sound. I grabbed Benjamin's arm to hold him still. By the looks of his face I could tell he had heard it, too. We rolled our eyes around the darkened living room.

Scratch, scratch.

"It's coming from behind those big stacks of newspapers," said Benjamin, switching on a table lamp.

"Hold it." I ran and got my flashlight from the kitchen and returned to the living room. I stood at the side of one of the newspaper towers and shone the flashlight between them and the wall.

"Any sign of them?" asked Benjamin.

"Nope." I pressed my head against the papers to reach farther back. The newspapers began to sway.

"Watch out!" exclaimed Benjamin. "The whole stack is about to—"

It all seemed to happen in slow motion. The newspapers arched across the length of the room and landed with a rumble that made the house shake.

"—fall," Benjamin finished.

"Did you get a glimpse of the cats?" I asked.

"They're long gone by now. Most animals can predict an earthquake."

I laughed. It was such a relief I kept on laughing. I put my hand behind the other stack of newspapers and gave it a shove. "Timmmmmmmmm-berrrrrrrrrrr!"

Benjamin gasped and leaped out of the way of the tumbling newspapers. "You maniac! What did you go and do that for?"

"For fun."

"Well, who do you think is going to clean them up?"

"We are," I said cheerfully. I picked up an armful of newspapers and started to stack them up again.

"Why just pile them up again?" asked Benjamin. "Why don't we do the Burrs a favor and recycle them? Montgomery Waste Company is currently paying four-fifty a ton for newspaper."

I let the newspapers fly. "What if the Burrs are saving them for something?"

"We'll call Mrs. Burr tomorrow and see."

"Good idea. Let's get out of here."

We locked up, then ran all the way home. Our comfy kitchen looked strange, like we had been away for years. I snatched my note off the kitchen table, crumpled it up, and tossed it into the wastebasket.

Wearily we climbed the stairs and said good night. In about two minutes, Benjamin was cutting the z's. I lay awake for a long time, too wound up to sleep. I happened to notice Tiffany's pony Oats set on the top shelf of my hutch. It was a good thing we took old Oats on. He was the only customer we had that didn't give us any trouble.

I started to doze when a scraping sound out in the garage made my eyes pop open. I rolled over and tried to go back to sleep. More noises came from the garage. I couldn't stand the suspense any longer. I got up and tiptoed downstairs. The kitchen door was ajar. I peeked through the crack into the garage. Mollie was bent over the freezer, a pile of frozen food at her feet.

I turned and ran upstairs. I leaped into bed and pulled the covers over my head. I braced myself for Mollie's scream.

It never came.

Chapter 11

Just between Mollie and Me

When I walked into the kitchen the next morning, Dad, dressed in his tennis whites, was eating breakfast with Benjamin. Mollie was dressed for tennis, too, in one of those dumb little skirts that shows your panties like a two-year-old. She was making an awful racket emptying the dishwasher. Silverware clattered, plates crashed, and pots and pans clanged. This was bad news. *I'm* supposed to empty the dishwasher. Whenever Mollie is really mad at me she does my chores. I think it's because she's afraid I won't do them, and she'll get even madder and explode into a zillion pieces.

"Hey there, Casey, congratulations!" said Dad. His face had that springy look from a good night's sleep. "I don't know what you did to old Ferdie, but you really got him to quiet down last night."

Benjamin's mouth was open for his next bite, but his hand had stopped in midair, halfway between his bowl and his mouth. I sure hoped he'd get his spoon moving again soon.

"I did hear someone in the garage about midnight," Dad continued. "Casey! Did you sneak that mutt into bed?"

"No, Daddy."

"Did you go out to see Ferdie last night, Benj?"

"No, Dad."

"Maybe you just heard Ferdie prowling around," I said.

Mollie slammed two pot lids together like she was the cymbal player in an orchestra. Dad's and Benjamin's spines snapped straight as rulers. I scrunched my shoulder up to my ear. "I am quite certain it was *not* Ferdie," she said.

Dad rolled his eyes toward Mollie. His face said: What are you so hysterical about? His mouth said, "What makes you think that, honey?"

Mollie stalked over to me. She laid her hand in the center of my back and nudged me toward the stairs. "Excuse us. We need to talk—woman to woman."

"Woman to woman?" echoed Dad. "Right now? Aren't we going to be late? Isn't Casey a little young?" You could tell he thought I was going to get the When You Grow into a Young Woman lecture.

I knew better. I stomped out of the kitchen ahead of Mollie. I was just about as mad as she was. It was no fair. Why was I the only one getting busted?

Mollie led me into her and Dad's bedroom and shut the door. She put her hands firmly on my shoulders and guided me to the bed. She pressed down until she and I were sitting side by side. Her hands on my shoulders melted into a hug. I was so relieved to just rest in her arms a moment. Ever since Ferdie died my head had gotten almost too heavy for my neck to hold it up.

"Oh, sweetheart," she exclaimed. "What happened?"

"Nothing. I mean, he just died in his sleep. Benjamin said it was natural causes, that it wasn't our fault."

"Of course not, dear," said Mollie. "But why did you put his body in the deep freeze with all our food?"

"So Mrs. Beasel could say good-bye to him. Ferdie was her companion in life. This will break her heart. Oh, Mollie, what will we ever tell her?"

"We'll tell her the truth, that's all. Try not to worry about it, Casey. We'll deal with it when the time comes. But right now, I want you and Benjamin to take that dog's carcass out of our freezer and bury it in the back-back." Her tone was calm enough, but it was also no-nonsense.

"But what about Daddy? When he finds out about this he'll make us stop our pet service."

"Never mind about Daddy until you get the dog buried. He'll be proud of you for taking on the responsibility."

I understood Mollie was making a deal with me. If I didn't tell Dad and Benjamin she cheated on her diet, she would stick up for me if Dad got upset about the Ferdie business. But I wasn't sure it was a fair deal. Maybe Dad wouldn't get upset. And I was pretty tired of Mollie trying to act like Ms. Perfect all the time. I crossed my arms and slid my eyes toward her. "Just what were you digging for at the bottom of the freezer in the middle of the night?"

Mollie pursed her lips and pulled her mouth to one side. Then she turned, took the box of Christmas chocolates out from under her pillow, and handed it to me. It was as light as a Frisbee.

"You ate the *whole* thing?" I asked.

Mollie removed the candy box lid. Among the empty brown ruffled papers were two lumpy pieces of chocolate. "Maple nut," she said. "Would you like them? They taste like shoe polish."

"No, thank you," I said politely. "I don't care much for shoe polish."

"You would think a dead dog carcass crushing the box would have ruined my appetite for chocolate. Obviously, it didn't." Mollie sighed. "I'm such a failure."

"Ah, no, you're not," I said. "If I was on that yucky diet for two weeks, I'd *kill* for chocolate."

There was a knock on the door. Mollie snatched the candy box out of my hands and slid it back under her pillow.

Dad poked his head into the room. "Is uh . . . has uh . . . everything been said in here? Woman to woman, I mean." His face turned tomato red.

Mollie laughed. "We're just finishing up. Come on in."

Dad and Benjamin shuffled in, looking the way they do when they have to sit through TV commercials for feminine protection.

Mollie clasped her hands together. "Casey and I were just discussing tonight's menu—barbecued hamburgers and corn on the cob."

"Ho-ho!" shouted Dad. He raised his pointed finger. "So you're going to blow the old diet after all."

"I wouldn't think of it," Mollie said demurely. "I've just decided to be a little more sensible about it."

"Can we have s'mores for dessert?" I asked.

"Certainly," said Mollie. "Anyone who can afford the calories. Personally, I prefer juicy, ice-cold watermelon."

"That sounds even better," I said. And it did, too.

"Now, run along, boys, I have one more thing to discuss with Casey." Mollie cupped her mouth with her hands and whispered, "The secret sauce."

She pushed Dad and Benjamin out of the room and shut the door with her bottom. "Casey," she said in a hushed voice, "I want to ask you a little favor." She nodded toward her pillow. "Will you dispose of the evidence?"

Maybe Mollie couldn't admit she wasn't perfect to Dad and Benjamin, but she could admit it to me. Usually she acted superior to my mom, but now she was taking her advice about sensible dieting. Besides all that, Dad was a ruthless kidder. I knew how much it hurt Mollie when he teased her about her diets and the little uncooked doughnut hanging around her waist. "Okay," I said. "I'll hide it way down in the garbage can underneath all the grass clippings. Dad and Benjamin will never find it."

Mollie gave me a hug. "Thanks, sweetie. Run along now. I need a moment of privacy."

When I got downstairs, I discovered that Benjamin had confessed to Dad about sneaking out of the house last night and about our little accident with the newspapers. Dad agreed to drive the van over to the Burrs's that afternoon so we could load up the newspapers and take them to the waste paper company.

After our parents left for the tennis courts, Benjamin called Mrs. Burr at her mother's house to make sure it was okay with her to haul the newspapers off. Meanwhile I sneaked into my parents' room and smuggled the candy box out under my T-shirt. I ran downstairs and out the back door. As I walked around the house toward the garbage can, I felt a tiny ache in my sweet tooth. I decided to at least try the shoe polish candies. I opened the box. It was empty.

Mollie had beaten me to them.

Chapter 12

A Resting Place for Ferdie

Benjamin and I selected a nice spot in the back-back for Ferdie's final resting place. It was underneath a gnarled old walnut tree with wide branches. In summer Ferdie would have cool shade. In fall he would be visited by squirrels scampering around collecting nuts. In winter the large sprawling branches would protect him from the rain. And in spring, new green leaves would sprout above his head.

I took the first turn at digging. The ground was real hard. After three shovelfuls of dirt, I was already panting. Sweat prickled my nape underneath my ponytail and little needles of pain stabbed my lower back.

Benjamin was lying on the grass. His hands were clasped behind his head and he was gazing up at the blue, cloudless sky. "I still can't figure out why you changed your mind."

"I can change my mind if I want."

"Sure you can. But what I want to know is why."

I leaned against the shovel handle and looked at Benjamin. "Sooner or later Dad and Mollie are going to notice Ferdie isn't around. It would be a lot easier to tell them he died if he's buried in the back-back rather than hiding out in the freezer."

"I agree," said Benjamin. "But there's still something weird about this. I should have been the one who thought of coming clean. I should have been more considerate about my mom's feelings. If she had happened to discover Ferdie in the freezer she would have screamed bloody murder and fainted dead away."

I started digging again so Benjamin couldn't read anything in my face. "Oh, I don't know. Mollie can be pretty cool about some things."

Benjamin bolted upright and pointed an accusing finger at me. "That's weird, too. You sticking up for Mom."

"Well, why wouldn't I? She is my stepmother."

"Now, I'm really worried. You in cahoots with Mom. What's up, Case?"

I straightened my arm and thrust the shovel handle into his hand. "Your turn, that's what. Dig, man, dig."

We switched off a few more times before we finished the hole. We got Ferdie out of the freezer and carried him out to the back-back. Neither of us said anything about unwrapping the plastic garbage bag and blanket to have a last look at him. I thought I would cry, but I didn't. That made me feel kind of guilty, like I didn't care about Ferdie, even though I really did. Benjamin was dry-eyed, too.

We placed the bundle in the hole and covered it up. Benjamin dumped the last load of dirt on top and packed it down with the back of the shovel. He leaned the handle against the walnut tree and slapped one palm against the other a couple of times. We stood side by side, looking down at Ferdie's grave.

"Well, that's that," said Benjamin.

"I guess so," I said, even though it didn't feel finished. "Hey, Benj, shouldn't we say something?"

"Oh, you mean like give Ferdie a funeral?"

"Yeah, like sort of a funeral. What do people do at funerals? I've never been to one."

"Me neither."

I held my elbow in my hand and rubbed underneath my ponytail. Sometimes rubbing the back of my brain helps me to think. "Well, we could say something nice about Ferdie."

"That's a good idea." Benjamin nudged my arm with his elbow. "You first."

I nudged him back. "No, you first."

"No, you. I can't think of anything good about him."

Benjamin nudged me harder, knocking my elbow out of my palm. The back of my left hand, dimpled with two purple spots, flopped in front of my face.

"Here lies Ferdie Beasel," I said. "He had good strong fangs."

"And an *excellent* appetite," said Benjamin.

"And a cute topknot . . . before I messed it all up with mousse."

"He was some kind of champion and won a lot of ribbons," said Benjamin. "At least, that's what Mrs. Beasel said."

"He was a good friend to Mrs. Beasel." My throat tightened, so that I nearly choked on my words. "Probably her best friend."

"Yes . . ." Benjamin's voice broke. "An excellent companion to Mrs. Beasel."

"And she'll be so sad when she finds out about this."

Finally the waterworks got going. Tears were running down both our cheeks.

"Oh, Benjamin, why did Ferdie have to go and die on us? I wish there was no such thing as death!"

"There's got to be." Benjamin touched his knuckle to the corner of his eye. "Or else all the people and dogs that ever lived would still be alive and there wouldn't be enough room for everything on earth."

"Cleopatra would still be around," I said.

"And John F. Kennedy and Einstein."

"Cavemen and dinosaurs." I snapped my head over my shoulder. The shadow of the walnut tree had suddenly turned into a towering brontosaurus about to stomp on us without even noticing we were there.

Benjamin went on, "And Attila the Hun and Hitler and Jack the Ripper."

"Owwww, stop!" A shiver ran through me and I hugged myself. By then I was glad there was such a thing as death.

"A part of Ferdie will still live on," said Benjamin.

"What do you mean?" I asked. "Where?"

Benjamin pointed to his head. "In Mrs. Beasel's memory.

Anytime she wants she can think back on the good times she had with him. It might make her sad, but she could be happy, too. She can feel what she felt when she was with him."

"I'll never forget Ferdie, either," I said. "I'm glad I got a chance to know him, even if it was for a short time."

By then we had stopped crying and were just sniffling.

"Now we need a marker," said Benjamin. "I can paint two boards white and nail them together to form a cross."

I imagined a white cross sticking up in the middle of our back-back and knew the front office wouldn't go for it. "Let's make the lying-down kind of marker, like in modern cemeteries. Mom says it's so lawn mowers can go over them."

"Those are made out of marble or bronze," said Benjamin. "Where would we get something like that?"

"We can use wood. You can write the words with your wood-burning kit. You can put: Here lies Ferdinand the Sixth, Best Friend and Beloved Companion to Mrs. Emma Beasel."

"I'll see what I can do," said Benjamin.

He went into the garage to get started on the marker while I worked a little more on the grave site. I gathered some white stones from our patio border and arranged them in a neat little rectangle around the perimeter of Ferdie's grave. I wanted to place some flowers on top of the mound of dirt, but the hot sun would have wilted them in a few minutes.

I got a soup can from the tin recycling bin in the garage. I dug a small hole at the head of Ferdie's grave and twisted the soup can down into it. I filled the can with water from the hose. I picked a bunch of bright orange, pink, and purple zinnias and placed them in the soup can.

Benjamin came out of the garage carrying a piece of plywood about the size of binder paper. He pushed it down in the dirt. He withdrew a whisk broom from his back pocket and swept the marker clean. It read:

FERDIE

Beloved Pet

"That's not what I said to put."

"Wood burning isn't so easy, you know," said Benjamin. "Besides, I had to write sort of big to make it look good."

"It does look good," I agreed.

"The white stones and flowers are a nice touch, too," said Benjamin.

It was a good thing we had done, a good deed. What we did that day would live on, just like everything else we would do in the future. When I grew up to be a big-animal veterinarian, I would become a part of the lives of all the people whose horses I helped. Maybe I would invent a new kind of horse care that would help horses I would never know personally. I thought of my life as a shiny red sports car going down a long, long highway. Then, when I died, the driver of the car would disappear, but the car would keep going, on and on and on.

"Good-bye, Ferdie," I said. "We'll never forget you."

Benjamin put his arm across his chest like he was saying the Pledge of Allegiance. "In our hearts, you will live on."

"And the trouble you caused us, too," I added.

Benjamin nodded. Neither of us mentioned it, but we were both thinking the same thing. We still had to tell Mrs. Beasel the bad news.

Chapter 13

The Mystery of Wilbur Burr

Monday morning Benjamin and I went over to the Burrs's to collect our money. We knocked on the back door and Mrs. Burr answered right away.

"Come in, kids," she said. "You did a great job of taking care of the cats. Wait here, I'll get my purse."

Wilbur was at the table eating a bowl of cereal and reading the back of the box. He pretended we weren't there so we did the same thing to him, even though it was hard because he slurped the milk off his spoon real loud.

Mrs. Burr returned. She handed us each a crisp five-dollar bill. "Keep the change, now. You deserve a little extra for hauling away all those old newspapers."

"Wow, we each get fifty cents extra," I said.

Benjamin scowled at me for being sarcastic to an adult,

but Mrs. Burr didn't even get it. She smiled and said, "Well, it's not much, just a little something."

"And Montgomery Waste Company paid us six twenty-five for the newspapers," said Benjamin.

"Hey, wait a minute." Wilbur pointed a finger at us and said, "Those were *our* newspapers. We should get at least half of that money."

Mrs. Burr slapped his outstretched wrist. "Nonsense, Sonny. Benjamin and Casey did us a big favor. You had your chance to haul off those papers, but you never could be bothered."

The corners of Wilbur's mouth started jumping up and down. "Well, I was *going* to do it. Now I can't."

"Nonsense," Mrs. Burr said again. She walked us to the door. "Thanks again, kids. If anyone asks me about pet care I'll be sure to recommend you."

"Thank you, Mrs. Burr," I said. "Good-bye."

I looked over at Benjamin, expecting him to say something polite, too, but he was red-faced and scowling. His arms were straight at his sides and his fists were clenched. As soon as Mrs. Burr closed the door, he exclaimed, "That creep!"

"Shhh!" I crossed my lips with my forefinger. "He'll hear you." I grabbed Benjamin's arm and pulled him along.

"I don't care if the *creep* does hear me." Benjamin turned his head and shouted the word *creep* toward the Burrs's house, even though by then we were out of earshot. "A grown man going after our hard-earned measly six bucks. What a jerk!"

"I feel sorry for him," I said.

"He's pathetic all right."

"No, I mean it. I always thought when you finally grew up you got to do anything you wanted. You could marry anybody you want. You could have any job, any car, any house. But if you're Wilbur Burr it doesn't look like you get diddly. What do you suppose went wrong with him?"

"Ah, he's just a lazy bum. Who cares?"

"No, Benjamin, there's more to it. Every day he gets up in that smelly house, lets his mother sew him ugly clothes, plays with his model trains, and . . . and what else? Don't you think one day he'd just get plain sick of it? One day he'd get up and decide to really *do* something?"

Benjamin shrugged. Wilbur Burr plainly didn't interest him one bit, but I couldn't stop thinking about him. I wondered if I could get to be a grown-up woman and still live in my same bedroom, with my horse statue collection on the top shelf of my hutch, Princess Jasmine on my bedspread, and Mollie downstairs screaming up at me about how many pairs of underwear I had worn that week.

Benjamin laughed. "I wonder how we did it."

I had no idea what he was talking about. "Did what?"

"How we managed to take such great care of the Burrs's cats without ever seeing them once."

I laughed, too. "I guess we're naturally talented."

We reached Barnett Circle. I saw Tiffany in her driveway skipping a kind of jump rope that made bubbles come out of the handles.

"Hey, when did you get back?" I asked.

"Back from where?" she asked.

"Back from your vacation."

"What vacation?"

I blew some air up into my bangs. "Didn't you ask us to take care of your so-called pony while you were away?"

"I never said I was going anywhere."

Benjamin and I exchanged looks. He shook his head and said, "Well, when do you want your old oatmeal box back?"

"What oatmeal box?"

"He means Oats, your pony," I said. "I'll go home and get him for you."

Tiffany stumbled over her rope. "You can't. I'm the one who gets to say when you give him back. You got to play fair or I'm telling my mom."

Benjamin laughed. "Look, Case. Taking care of a dumb old oatmeal box while she's in town makes about as much sense as taking care of it while she's out of town."

"Oats is not neither an oatmeal box," said Tiffany. "I'm telling what mean things you said."

"Go ahead, big tattletale," I said. "See what we care."

Late that afternoon, while Benjamin was looking for fish spots and I was wondering what to do about plant spots, Tiffany and her mother came by our house.

When we answered the door, Mrs. Levitsky blurted out, "If you kids don't stop teasing Tiffany I'm telling your parents."

I raised my eyebrows up to my bangs. I had never heard of an adult tattletale.

Mrs. Levitsky went on. "Tiffany says you took away the little dog she made in arts and crafts."

"It's a pony," I said. "She asked us to take care of it for her."

Mrs. Levitsky crossed her arms. "A likely story. Go get it."

I ran upstairs, snatched Oats off my hutch, and returned it to Tiffany. "Three days, five cents a day, that will be fifteen cents, please," I said.

We all looked at one another for a while until Mrs. Levitsky got impatient. "So give Tiffany the fifteen cents."

"What?" I said. "She's supposed to give *us* the money."

"That's preposterous," said Mrs. Levitsky. "You told my daughter you'd pay her to let you play with the toy."

"No, see, we have this pet care service," I began, "and we charge—"

Mrs. Levitsky bent down and roared into my face, "You charge little kids for keeping their oatmeal boxes?"

Benjamin dug a whole wad of stuff out of his pocket, picked out a dime and a nickel, and handed them to Tiffany. "Here ya go. A deal's a deal."

"Now just a darn minute," I sputtered.

"Bye, Mrs. Levitsky, bye Tif." Benjamin shut the door and leaned against it, his arms crossed over his chest. "Believe me, Case, it's just easier this way."

Chapter 14

My Previous Life

The rest of the week I felt like Benjamin and I were in a car wreck about to happen. We were bound for a collision with Mrs. Beasel when she got home. Usually you don't know you're going to be in a car wreck very far in advance. You brace yourself against the dashboard and squeeze your eyes shut for maybe a couple of seconds. But for me, that tight, tense feeling stretched on day after day after day.

Whenever the phone rang I jumped. It felt like I was connected to the ringer with an invisible cord that jolted me with an electrical shock every time we got a call. I hoped Mrs. Beasel would phone to say she had decided to stay and live in Missoura and we could keep Ferdie; so then we wouldn't have to tell her you know what. I hoped my mom would call to say she got the part of the tomato after all, or some other vegetable, so she could now afford my airline ticket. I guess there's such a thing as hoping too much.

Benjamin spent most of his time peering into Terminal's goldfish bowl, spot-checking for Ich. I spent my time caring for Mrs. Singer's plants. I fed them and watered them and pinched off their dead leaves. I also talked to them a lot. It's suppose to console them and make them grow better. It seemed to console me, too. I found I actually liked taking care of the plants, except for the fact that I couldn't make the brown spots on the Rabbit Tracks Maranta disappear. I hoped Mrs. Singer wouldn't blame me for them. By Sunday I was still wondering what to do about them.

"I just have to keep ole Terminal alive one more day," Benjamin said happily.

"That fish doesn't have anything wrong with him," I said. "Who cares about an old Bristol Shubunkin goldfish anyway? I wish he had died instead of Ferdie."

"Thanks a lot. You want Bradley to pound me?"

I didn't reply. I was so miserable I didn't even feel like fighting with Benjamin. I shuffled out of the room and trudged up the stairs. I threw myself on my bed and covered my eyes in the crook of my arm.

There was a timid knock on my door and Benjamin walked in. He hung around not saying anything.

Finally I sat up and started whining. "If only my idiot mom would've let me come visit like she was supposed to then we'd never have to face Mrs. Beasel. I'll never be able to raise the money for an airline ticket. I may never see my mom again and I'm not even sure she cares." I didn't know

I was going to say any of this. The words came rushing out of my mouth like a train out of a tunnel.

"Why don't you call your mom and tell her how you feel?"

"I'd just get her dumb old answering service."

"Then write her a letter."

"I write her letters all the time. Except . . ." I got off my bed and went to the wastebasket. I got out all my reject letters one by one and smoothed them out on the desk.

"You just throw them away? You don't send them?"

"I don't sent her *these*. These tell the truth. What I send her is a pack of lies."

"But why?"

"Writing isn't like talking, you know. You can write things, then have time to take them back. I write her about all my mean, bad feelings, and troubles, and then toss them out. Then I start over and write only good things." One tear rolled down my cheek and I swiped at it. "So she'll like me. So she'll want to have me around."

"She probably loves you no matter what you write," said Benjamin. "It's a built-in, survival-of-the-species thing."

"Then she should find a way for me to come visit."

"How does she know what you really want if you don't tell her the truth? Maybe she thinks it's just fine with you that you're not coming to see her."

"I don't know what she thinks. I just know Dad and her and me were having a great life together one day and the next day—poof—she was gone."

"Maybe your dad could help you with this."

"I don't think your mom likes my dad talking about my mom, and she's always around."

"You can get your dad off to yourself if you want to. I could get Mom busy doing something with me."

"You will?" I looked toward Benjamin, but instead of him I saw Dad's face, tight and angry, the way it used to get whenever I asked anything about Mom. I had given it up long ago, before Mollie even arrived on the scene.

"Just say when," said Benjamin.

"I'm sort of afraid to," I said. "Maybe he would say mean things about her because he doesn't love her anymore."

"Or maybe he would tell you the plain truth. But you know, Case, sometimes the truth hurts."

"Does it ever," I said.

Benjamin went into his room and closed the door. I lay back on my bed to think things over some more. Then another idea struck me like a lightning bolt.

I got my green mint-scented marker out of my desk and went down to the family room. I colored in all the brown spots on the Rabbit Tracks Maranta. I put it in one of Mrs. Singer's cardboard boxes and loaded up a bunch of other plants in front of it. I packed up the other plants and supplies, all ready to take back in the morning.

That night while we all watched TV, Dad, Mollie, and Benjamin burst out laughing, and I didn't even know what was so funny. I couldn't concentrate, thinking about my talk with Dad. I bumped Benjamin's shoulder with mine. He looked at me like was I trying to start something. Then he remembered our deal.

"Oh, uh, Mom, come see Bradley's fish," said Benjamin. "Did you know he was a genuine Bristol Shubunkin?"

"Oh, Benj, I've seen that silly fish a hundred times." Mollie laughed at the show again.

"Then come see the plants." Benjamin grabbed Mollie's hand and tried to pull her up off the sofa.

"Benjamin, stop. I want to see my show."

Benjamin let go of his mom's hand and gave me an apologetic look. I couldn't blame him. He tried.

I started roaming around the house, too restless to sit any longer. I missed my mom. I wanted to see her. I wanted to feel closer to her. Suddenly I thought of our old red photo album.

I switched on the light in Dad's office. The wall behind his big computer table was lined with bookshelves. I crawled under the table and looked on the far left of the lowest bookshelf.

It was so dark back there, I couldn't see colors. I pulled two photo albums off the shelf. They were the heavy three-ringed binder type with plastic pockets to put pictures in. I crept out from under the desk. In the light, I discovered I had the red album I was looking for and a green one that I had never seen. I lugged both albums to Dad's old La-Z-Boy recliner and flicked on the reading light. I sank down into the big chair and opened the red album.

There were about a zillion pictures of me when I was a baby and little kid. Flipping through the pages, I watched myself grow from zero to four in about a minute. One picture was of some little kids dressed in Little Red Riding Hood costumes. There was a Little Red Riding Hood, a grandmother, a wolf, and a hunter. You couldn't tell who was inside the wolf costume, but I knew it was me. At the time the picture was taken, my mom ran a day care center in our house. "Showtime" was her favorite game to play with us kids.

In the next twenty or so pages, I grew a head taller and lost most of my teeth. One picture was of my dad and mom, posing in swimsuits before blue and green Lake Tahoe. They looked like they were leaning off to the side, about to fall over, but I knew that was because I had snapped the picture. Dad had his arm around Mom's waist and they were looking into each other's eyes. Underneath the picture, Mom had written, "Jack and Jackie in love." I felt sad and mad all at the same time. How could two married people named Jack and Jackie ever get a divorce?

There weren't many more pages after that, and I flipped through them fast. Then I looked in the green album. The opening pages held a series of photographs of a big fancy house under construction. First there was just a slab of cement and then a wooden frame. Next came plumbing and wiring. A roof of red-curved tiles was put on and the walls were filled in.

I turned the page and saw the finished house. Then it hit me like a ton of bricks. I had lived in that house! It was the house my mom ran away from.

I flipped the pages with shaking fingers. The next page had no pictures on it. The next page after that was blank, too. I kept turning the empty pages, knowing I wouldn't find any more pictures. The story of my previous life with

Mom and Dad had ended, even though I wanted it to go on and on. I reached the final page of the green album and closed it.

I got up and crawled back under the desk to return the albums. A tall skinny book was wedged diagonally in the space where they belonged. I pulled it out and returned the albums. Replacing the thin book, I tilted it so that the cover caught a wedge of light. It read: EL CAMINO HIGH SCHOOL, SACRAMENTO, CALIFORNIA, CLASS OF '79. I knew it was my parents' yearbook.

I brought it to the easy chair and looked through it. I found a big picture of my mom performing in a show. Her blond hair was long and tied in pigtails with big comical bows. She wore a gingham dress with a full skirt and big puffy sleeves, like an old-fashioned country girl. She was bent at the waist with her hands on her knees. Her eyes were big and rolled to the side. Her mouth was so wide open, I could tell she was singing.

A sharp rap on the door made me jump. I slammed the book shut over my forefinger. Dad stuck his head in.

"Oh, Casey, we were just wondering what you were— oh, gosh! My high school yearbook!"

Dad walked in. He picked me up and set me on his lap. He opened the yearbook where I had marked my place with my finger. I leaned against his chest and looked up at his face, watching him look at Mom's picture.

His eyebrows shot up and he smiled big. "Hey, there's your mom in *Oklahoma*. She brought the house down."

"Was she the star?" I asked.

"Not exactly. It's called the supporting role. She played Ado Annie—a silly girl who likes to kiss all the boys. She sings a very funny song called 'I Cain't Say No.' " Dad's smile melted away. "That's your mother, all right."

I was horrified. "Mom liked to kiss all the boys?"

Dad chuckled. "No. I mean the 'I Cain't Say No' part. She should have said no to a lot of things."

"Like what?"

"Like getting married so young. But that was my fault. I kept bugging her and bugging her until she finally agreed to marry me. What she really wanted to do was go to college and major in drama. She had won a scholarship to UCLA."

"If you knew that's what she really wanted to do, why didn't you let her?"

Dad shrugged. "I was afraid if I let her go to Los Angeles by herself she'd meet someone else and I'd lose her."

Neither of us said anything for a while. We both knew he had lost her anyway. Finally I said, "I was looking through some photo albums. I forgot about that big fancy house we lived in for a while."

Dad sighed. "That's another thing your mom should've said no to. The plan was for her to work while I went to college; then when I graduated, I would go to work and she could go to college. But, ten years later, by the time I landed my first high-paying job, your mom had stopped talking about becoming an actress. I figured she was happy just being a mom and a wife. I wanted to give her a very special present—a custom-built dream house."

"What a rip-off!" I exclaimed. "Instead of getting to be an actress she gets a big dumb old house."

"I should have known better. Whenever she wanted something that I didn't, we'd talk and talk until I talked her into doing things my way. I guess finally she stopped talking about what she wanted and just went ahead and did it."

"And now she hardly ever sees me, her very own daughter. Is that what she wants?"

"No, I'm sure that makes her very sad. I know she loves you more than anybody and she misses you very much."

I nestled against Dad and he held me tight. Just then Mollie appeared at the door. "What's up, guys?" She looked us over and added timidly, "Oh, am I interrupting something?"

I wanted to say she was, but Dad said, "Oh, not at all. You'll never guess what Casey dug up! My high school yearbook."

"Oh, let me see you, you handsome devil." Mollie walked over and sat on the arm of the big chair. She looked down and said, "Oh, isn't that Jackie?"

"Uh-huh," said Dad.

I expected Mollie to say something mean or act jealous. Instead she laughed and clapped her hands. "Wasn't she a doll! No wonder you fell for her hook, line, and sinker."

"I'll show you where I am," said Dad. He started to turn the page, but Mollie placed her hand on his. "Wait, let me see." She stared at my mom's picture a long moment. "You know, Casey, there's a lot of your mother in you."

"Oh, I don't look at all like her," I said. "Everyone always says I'm the spitting image of Dad."

"There's some of your mom in you, too. It's becoming more apparent as you grow older. Don't you think, Jack?"

Mollie pointed to my mom's face. "See that glint in her eye, that set chin, that look of determination."

Dad laughed. "I see it, all right."

Then Mollie laughed, too.

I narrowed my eyes and looked at them hard.

"It's a good thing, Casey," Mollie assured me. "I'm proud of your tenacity, honey. You just have to learn to accept responsibility for your actions."

There was that word *responsibility* again, rearing its ugly head. I imagined its face was green with bumpy black warts.

Mollie stroked my mother's picture with one fingertip. "I bet you'll look a lot like this when you're in high school, sweetie. I bet you'll knock 'em dead."

"Well, I just hope I don't have to wait till high school before I get to see my mom again."

I looked up from my mom's picture and saw Mollie and Dad staring at each other over the top of my head. Dad raised one eyebrow and tucked his chin against his throat, like he was asking Mollie a question. She replied with one quick nod.

"I don't believe we've been fair to you, Casey," said Dad. "A girl needs to see her mother. Mollie and I will pay for your airline ticket."

"Oh, Daddy, do you mean it?" I threw my arms around his neck, knocking into Mollie's hand, which was draped over his shoulder, and gave him a big smacker on the cheek.

"Hold on, now," said Dad. "I'm wondering if your mother can handle the rest of your expenses. There's food and—"

"Oh, I don't eat much," I said.

"And child care," continued Dad, "and any number of things. It's not cheap, you know."

"I've earned a little money with the Casey Wooster's Pet Care and Grooming Service."

"Good for you, Casey," said Mollie. "And your daddy and I will cover whatever else you need."

I hugged her, too. "Oh, thank you! Thank you, so much!"

I ran up to my room to write my mom the good news.

Hey, Mom,

You'll never guess what! Dad and Mollie said I can come visit you after all. They'll pay for it. Isn't that the greatest?

Still I think it's really crummy you didn't have the money to send for me. Dad and Mollie are right—it's your responsibility. I think you should not have bought some stuff, even some of the stuff you gave me. Please, please don't ever forget to save money for my visits ever again. I came so close to not seeing you this summer it's almost scary.

I was trying to earn money for my own airline ticket. That's why I started the Casey Wooster's Pet Care and Grooming Service I told you about. The reason our first customer is not feeling very good is because he's dead. (Natural causes.) Benjamin and I still have to tell Mrs. Beasel when she comes home next week. I'm real worried about breaking the news to her. I'll be so relieved when it's over.

Tonight I saw a picture of you as Ado Annie in your high

school yearbook. I understand better now why you ran away. You didn't run *from* me so much as you ran *to* being an actress. If something told me I would never be a big-animal veterinarian and never get to own my own horse, not ever in my whole life, I think I might run away, too.

Mollie says I'm starting to look like you. She says it's a good thing. Mollie is turning out to be an okay person. As long as I have to have a stepmother I'm glad it's her.

Call me or write me soon and tell me when is the best time for me to arrive. I can't wait to see you. I love you so much.

Love,
Casey Wooster

I put the letter in an envelope, and stamped and addressed it. I went outside, even though it was dark and creepy. I ran down to the corner mailbox, dropped the letter in, and raced home. I was panting hard by the time I stepped back inside.

I was too excited to wait for my letter to reach my mom so I gave her a call. Of course, I got her dumb old answering service. I left my message: I'm coming to visit after all!

Chapter 15
Relief

Bright and early the next morning, Benjamin and I put the plants, supplies, and fish into his old red wagon and carefully wheeled it down to Bradley's house.

When Bradley answered the door he said, "You mean you didn't kill my fish?" He seemed almost disappointed.

Mrs. Singer came up behind him. "Hi, kids. The plants look great." She stopped to lift one of the boxes out of the wagon and sniffed. "Something smells minty. I don't have any mint plants."

"Are you sure this is my fish?" said Bradley. "It doesn't look like my fish. I bet mine died and you replaced it with a another one."

"It looks exactly like your fish," said Mrs. Singer. "Come in, Benjamin and Casey. I'll write you a check."

We helped her carry in the rest of the plants and supplies. Bradley took in the fishbowl. He tripped over a throw rug and went sprawling. The bowl bounced on the carpet and the fish got beached on the coffee table.

"Quick, do something," cried Benjamin. "He's dying."

Mrs. Singer came calmly to the rescue with a cereal bowl of water. She squatted down and scooped the fish into it. "This happens all the time. Bradley can't keep a fish alive a single week. He's always dropping them, losing them down the drain, or forgetting to feed them. I think this will be the last one. It's too painful to watch."

Bradley rubbed his knee and scowled at his mother. "You don't even care if I broke my leg, you're so worried about that dumb fish." He got up and limped dramatically toward his room.

On the way home, Benjamin happily waved Mrs. Singer's check in the breeze, letting the ink dry. I wondered how such a nice lady got stuck with such a rotten kid.

When we got back, Jenny still wasn't there. That gave us a chance to go into the living room and play Hot Lava. We try to make it all the way around the room without touching the carpet. Benjamin was perched on the bookcase, and I had one foot on the sofa and the other on the coffee table when the doorbell rang.

"Time out," said Benjamin. He leaped to the floor.

"Hot lava, you're dead," I said.

"I said time out," he yelled.

The coffee table slipped farther away from the sofa. I was just about doing the splits in midair before I fell and landed on my bottom.

"Ha-ha, I won," said Benjamin.

"Cheater! You can't win on a time out."

The doorbell rang again. We both ran to the door and slammed against it. We started giggling. I opened the door, expecting to find Jenny. As soon as we saw who it was, we stopped laughing. Benjamin about popped a contact lens.

"I know I should have called first, but I was so excited to see my Ferdie, I dashed right over here as soon as I got home." Mrs. Beasel was wearing thongs, baggy Bermuda shorts, an oversized T-shirt with THE SHOW-ME STATE written on it, and a straw hat with little orange balls dangling off the wide brim. Slung over her arm was a large beach bag that matched her hat. She looked like she had had a great time in Missoura.

"Aren't you a little early?" asked Benjamin.

"Just a few days. I got to missing my little pal so much I just had to come back."

Suddenly all my courage drained out through my toes. I didn't mean to lie, I just couldn't face the truth. "You'll have to come back later," I stalled. "Ferdie isn't quite ready to pick up."

"What do you mean, not ready?"

"I mean, well, we're going to slick him up some. Give him a bath and all and—"

"That's not it!" Benjamin wriggled under my arm to stand between Mrs. Beasel and me. "The fact is . . ."

"Did he get out of the yard?" exclaimed Mrs. Beasel. "Don't tell me you lost him!"

I shoved Benjamin away and swung the door wide open. "Please, come in out of the heat, Mrs. Beasel." She stepped inside and I shut the door. "Have a seat." I extended my arm toward the sofa. I noticed my dusty footprint. "Oops. Excuse me." I brushed off the sofa. "Now, have a seat. Let me get you some ice-cold orange juice."

"No, thank you," said Mrs. Beasel. "I'm anxious to see my Ferdie. Now is he here or not?"

"He's sort of here," said Benjamin.

"And he's sort of not," I added.

Mrs. Beasel looked at me, then Benjamin, then me again. Her eyebrows ran together over the top of her nose. "Are you children playing a game with me?"

"No, ma'am," I said. My heart was thumping so wildly, I looked down, expecting to see my T-shirt jumping. "I'm afraid we have some bad news for you."

"Has something happened to Ferdie? Is he sick? Did you have to take him to the vet?"

I shook my head. "I think you better come with us."

Benjamin and I led Mrs. Beasel through the kitchen and out to the backyard. She took slow plodding steps, fanning herself with her hat.

"Are you feeling okay, Mrs. Beasel?" I asked.

"I'm fine, dear. Just show me where Ferdie is."

We led her to the back-back. Luckily that morning I had put fresh zinnias in the soup can. I had swept the FERDIE plaque and straightened the white rocks bordering the grave.

Mrs. Beasel took one look and put her face in her hands. She made a "hoo-hoo" sound sort of like an owl, only higher pitched.

Benjamin and I looked at each other. It was the worst moment in our lives.

"Go get a lawn chair off the patio," I said.

Benjamin ran out the gate. I wished I had something to do, too. It was scary just standing there with Mrs. Beasel. She was the loudest crier I ever heard. I was tempted to stick my fingers into my ears, but I knew how impolite that would be. Benjamin brought the chair into the back-back and opened it up.

"Would you like to sit down?" I asked.

She didn't seem to hear me. I placed my hand on her elbow and tried to steer her into the chair, but she didn't budge. I guess she didn't feel like sitting down and it seemed safe for her to keep standing. She sounded too loud for a person about to faint.

"Ferdie didn't suffer or anything," I said. "He just went to sleep and never woke up. We're really, really sorry."

"We'll try to make it up to you," said Benjamin.

"Hoo-hoo!" Mrs. Beasel cried even louder.

"I know a new dog wouldn't be the same as Ferdie," I said, "but . . . hey, we could come visit you if you want somebody to talk to about him. That is, if you can stand the sight of us."

"Of course, I'd be grateful for your company!" Mrs. Beasel let one handle of her beach bag slide off her arm so that it dangled wide open. She withdrew a Kleenex and blew her nose with a loud honk-honk. "You poor, sweet children," she exclaimed.

"Oh, we're not poor," I said. "We just feel so bad for you. We know you loved old Ferdie a whole lot."

"Old is right," said Mrs. Beasel. "I never should have left him with you. What you must have gone through! This would have been so much easier for the kennel to handle. But"—she smiled through her tears—"I'm glad I did."

"You are?" I asked.

"I'm so touched. This is a beautiful resting place for Ferdie. I bet he likes it, too. I'll bet he's in doggie heaven right now, beaming down at us."

I didn't actually believe in doggie heaven, but I didn't tell that to Mrs. Beasel. If it made her feel any better, that was fine with me. People have a right to believe what they want.

"Thank you, Casey, thank you, Benjamin." Mrs. Beasel hugged us in turn. She reached into her purse and drew out her wallet. She handed each of us several bills.

"We can't take your money," said Benjamin.

"Oh yes, you can. I was prepared to pay much more than that to the Doggie Haven Cemetery. And I think you children gave Ferdie a much more caring send-off than they ever would."

"It's the least we could do," I said. "We don't want any money for it."

Benjamin and I extended the bills toward Mrs. Beasel, but she waved them away. "I've been in such a dither for some time now, stewing over all the arrangements. You've handled everything beautifully. I feel so relieved now."

"I'm just glad you're not mad at us," I said. "I was afraid you would think Ferdie died because we didn't take good enough care of him."

"Goodness, no." Mrs. Beasel smiled sweetly. "He had a good, long, happy life. His time was up, that's all."

We walked her to her car. We waved until she drove out of sight.

"Phew!" said Benjamin, dramatically sweeping the back of his hand across his forehead.

"Phew is right!"

I elbowed Benjamin. He elbowed me back. I backhanded his shoulder. He slugged my arm. We started laughing. We laughed and laughed.

"Stop! Stop!" I begged. "I'm going to pee in my pants." I ran into the house and went to the bathroom. When I came out Benjamin was tightrope-walking over the arm of an easy chair. I sat down on the sofa.

"Play ya another game of Hot Lava," he said.

"Naw, I'm thinking."

Benjamin slid into the chair and hung upside down like an opossum. "About what?"

"Going out of business."

"Good idea," said Benjamin.

"And starting a new one."

"Uh-oh. What is it this time?"

"How does Casey Wooster's Pet Cemetery sound to you?"

"Sick. The front office isn't going to go for a lot of dead bodies hanging around in the back-back. Besides, you're going to be gone all summer now."

"We can work on the cemetery when I get back in the fall."

"You're out of your mind. This is the most mercenary scheme I've ever heard you come up with."

"What's mercenary?" I asked.

"Doing something you don't like to do just to make money."

"I knew that."

"You don't even need to pay for your airline ticket now."

I rested my chin on my knuckle. "Hmm . . . that's true. Now I can start saving for a horse."

Benjamin groaned. "Here we go again."

I grinned. That meant I could count him in.

The telephone rang. I jumped, forgetting I didn't have to jump anymore. My worries were over. I went into the kitchen and answered the phone.

"Honey, it's me," said Mom. "I got your wonderful message. How'd you ever swing it?"

"Daddy and Mollie had a change of heart. They said they'd pay for my airline ticket, after all."

"If they can pay half, I can pay half," said Mom.

"We can split it three ways," I said. "I've earned some money with my pet care service."

"Oh, how is that going?"

"Great. Benj and I just decided to go out of business. Disneyland here I come."

"I've got a two-week paid vacation coming up at Jiffy Lube when we can do all the tourist stuff," said Mom. "The rest of your visit you'll be attending the Sheridan School for Performing Arts. They have everything: singing, dancing, fencing. You'll be just crazy about it."

I wasn't so sure about that. This sounded like all the stuff my mom was interested in. I had never even tried to build a fence. I didn't want to hurt my mom's feelings so I said, "That sounds real expensive."

"Oh, it's exorbitant!" exclaimed Mom. "But you're going for free. Sunny Sheridan and I made a swap. I keep her car in tip-top running order—it's a classic, she won't trust it with just any mechanic—and in return she's giving you free tuition for summer session. Oh, and there's Mustang—you and she are going to be the very best of friends."

This sounded too good to be true. "Sunny has a horse? I'm going to get to ride her?"

"What? No, darling, not a horse, a daughter. Haven't you ever heard of Mustang Sheridan? She has her own series on daytime TV. She's quite a talented little actress, but, just between you and me, you've got a lot more spark. Sunny named her after her car, the one I take care of. It's a sixty-five Mustang. Just darling."

Now I was confused. Was Mustang the car just darling or Mustang the girl? My mom had gotten so used to talking fast on other people's phones that it was hard for me to understand her. After I hung up, the inside of my head was singing like I had ridden the Whirling Lobster Ride about a dozen times in a row.

Benjamin dashed into the kitchen. "Well, how was it? Did she seem excited you were coming?"

"Yeah," I said vaguely, still trying to sort through the conversation. "Mom says I'm going to be friends with a TV star my age. Mustang Sheridan."

Benjamin wrinkled his nose. "Oh, boy. You ever notice when a parent says you're going to get along great with some other kid, you find out you just can't stand them?"

I thought a moment, then shrugged. "Oh well, if we don't like her we can just ditch her."

"What do you mean 'we'? I'm not going with you."

Lately, I had gotten so used to having Benjamin around that when I imagined Disneyland, Dodgers' games, and Santa Monica Beach, he was always right there in the picture.

"What's wrong, Case? You sick or something? Your face looks like it got left in the freezer too long. What's this Mustang Sheridan's show called anyway—'My Daughter the Car'?" He held his belly and hooted.

I stuck my tongue out at him. He countered with the ghoul face he makes by pulling down his cheeks to show the red part of his eyes and pushing up his nose to show his boogers. I yanked his white-blond antenna, then ran upstairs and into my room. I shut the door, locked it, then leaned against it. Benjamin slammed against the opposite side of the door, a split second too late.

"Ha-ha, didn't catch me," I sang out.

"You just wait, I'll get you yet," said Benjamin.

I took one deep breath, enjoying the glory of being one up, then shivered deliciously, wondering how I would have to pay for it later.

Then I started packing.